Guest Night

ON

Union Station

EarthCent Ambassador Series:

Date Night on Union Station

Alien Night on Union Station

High Priest on Union Station

Spy Night on Union Station

Carnival on Union Station

Wanderers on Union Station

Vacation on Union Station

Guest Night on Union Station

Word Night on Union Station

Party Night on Union Station

Review Night on Union Station

Family Night on Union Station

Book Night on Union Station

LARP Night on Union Station

Book Eight of EarthCent Ambassador

Guest Night on Union Station

Foner Books

ISBN 978-1-948691-10-9

Northampton, Massachusetts

One

"In conclusion, it is the view of Union Station Embassy that our back-to-back hosting of the Third Annual Conference of Sovereign Human Communities and the upcoming Stryx open house is well within our capabilities, and I consider it an honor to be chosen as hostess for the latter event."

Kelly cut short the final sentence of her weekly report to avoid running out of breath, and then she mentally tallied up the number of words in her conclusion. The ambassador had been informed by the president himself that students in the EarthCent diplomacy school had invented a drinking game based on word count of the final sentence in her weekly reports. Now she felt guilty if the report fell short of fifty words.

It seemed to Kelly that she had lost lung capacity since turning fifty, though Joe assured her it was just her imagination. To get back into shape, she'd begun leaving early for work every day and exiting the lift tube in the Little Apple, a brisk fifteen-minute walk from the embassy. That the exercise course took her by Hole Universe, home of the triple-chocolate donut, may have been related to the counterintuitive weight gain she was experiencing, but the ambassador wasn't one to rush to judgment.

1

"An honor to be chosen?" Libby's voice interrupted Kelly's thoughts. "As the ambassador of the latest species to join the tunnel network and maintain an embassy on this station, hosting the open house is a duty spelled out in the End User License Agreement for your diplomatic implant."

"You should change your name to Eula, you love bringing it up so much," Kelly retorted. "Anyhow, there's no rule that says a duty can't be an honor as well. Which species hosted the last open house on Union Station?"

"The Chert. Unfortunately, they were still in hiding at the time and their ambassador refused to turn off his invisibility projector. In the end, none of the invited guests signed up for the tunnel network, though to be fair, most of our open houses fail to close the deal."

"You mean the aliens who show up are just window shopping?"

"The tunnel network is a bit of a hard sell for species who are accustomed to living independently, but that's why we're so hopeful about this coming event. These guests will all be from the Cayl Empire, which is peacefully winding down operations after seven million years. The member species are already habituated to living with a higher authority."

"Who winds down an empire?" Kelly demanded. "I've never heard of such a thing. Do you mean to say that the Cayl went bankrupt and they've gone into receivership? How can anybody collect a debt from a military power?"

"The Cayl finances are in no worse shape than usual, but it appears that the emperor has simply lost interest in being in charge," Libby explained. "There aren't many commercial ties between the tunnel network species and the Cayl Empire because the distances involved make shipping without tunnel connections too expensive, but we've always kept communications open at the highest level. The Cayl are the archetypal warrior/scientist species. They were never interested in accumulating wealth and considered trade to be beneath their dignity, which is one of the secrets to what makes their empire work."

"Ignoring business is healthy for an imperial government? But that's the exact opposite of the Stryx approach."

"If you're going to dominate other species militarily, as the Cayl do, it's important to give something back. The Cayl's distaste for all things related to commerce made them the poor men of their own empire. Some of the subjugated species have piled up fortunes by overcharging their conquerors for goods and services. The Cayl disdain anything to do with money, and it's a truism in the empire that a Cayl warrior would never buy a drink in a bar if he could pay more at the bar next door."

"So why didn't all of those defeated aliens get together and use the money to build fleets or hire mercenaries to win back their independence?"

"And kill the goose that lays the golden eggs? It didn't take long for any of the species the Cayl fought to realize it was more profitable to surrender and become part of the empire. Once the word got out, most of them only put up a token show of fighting to satisfy honor on both sides."

"Well, if that's the case, I guess it makes sense that those species would be shopping for a new protector. But what made the Cayl finally quit the game?"

"Brawn-drain," Libby replied. "Although military training is part of their culture, most of the Cayl would rather spend their time doing scientific research than babysitting an empire, which is entirely understandable. The Cayl have built a unique society in many ways, but they've grown tired of always being the adult in the room."

"So that's it? They packed their bags and walked away from their own empire?"

"The member species needed time to decide on an alternative, so they took up a collection to hire the Cayl war fleets and garrisons to extend their stay. It's actually the best bit of business to come the Cayl's way in eons, but the emperor insisted on setting a departure date that's fast approaching. It also means that we should have some motivated buyers on our hands."

"So you're setting up a temporary tunnel and inviting representatives from all of those species to visit Union Station in order to wow them with what they'll get if they join up," Kelly summarized.

"Yes, though in practice, there's no one-size-fits-all sales pitch," Libby explained. "For example, the Verlocks signed up so they could scale back their military spending, while the Vergallians were more interested in freeing up resources to extend their reach outside of the tunnel network. In truth, accepting the Vergallians was a bit of an experiment that we're still assessing."

"How about the Hortens?"

"The Hortens joined for the Stryxnet, which is to say, they had run out of bandwidth for some of the massive multi-user games they play. The Drazens joined because they were allies with the Hortens back then and they were impressed by the food courts on our stations. Both the Grenouthians and the Dollnicks joined for expanded market opportunities, and Chert, as you know, are refugees."

"Can you give some examples I'd recognize of the species that turned you down?"

4

"Although we enforce very few laws related to commercial transactions, the Sharf didn't like the fact that we regulate the new and used spaceship dealerships on the stations. Before Gryph and the others introduced that law, the station bots spent half of their time out on search-and-rescue missions for careless shoppers who blew all of their money on a lemon and couldn't afford to pay for a tow to save their lives. We even offered the Sharf an exemption if they would just pay for search-and-rescue on their own ship sales, but their dealership lobby was too powerful."

"How about the Farlings?"

"I don't think they believe we have anything to offer them, and they subscribe to the thesis that we favor humanoid species, despite all of the evidence to the contrary. They also nurse a grudge against the first generation Stryx for bringing an end to the Farling military expansion phase a long time ago, even before we exiled the Brupt for attacking our member species."

Kelly continued to run through the other aliens she dealt with on a day-to-day basis, excusing her curiosity as being educational for her upcoming role as the open house hostess. "What did you offer the Frunge and the Gem?"

"The Frunge were won over by our willingness to reengineer space for them on the stations. It's not obvious when you visit, but between the height of some of their ancestral trees and the depth of the root structures, we had to take out a floor and give them a double deck. And the Gem joined because we were willing to accept them at a time when all of the other species shunned them for being clones."

"So if five species from the Cayl Empire end up sending representatives, it could take ten different reasons to bring them all on board," Kelly mused. "Still, if they're willing to come all the way here, they must be pretty interested."

"We aren't their only option, and it's not every day that an intact empire comes on the galactic market. They'll want to shop us against the alternatives, and there will certainly be a faction that will promote forming a confederation, rather than finding a new protector."

"What alternatives? One of the off-tunnel species like the Sharf or the Farlings?"

"The galaxy is much larger than the systems on our tunnel network and their immediate neighbors," Libby reminded her human friend. "There are dozens of empires of roughly the same scale as the Cayl. None of them would need to maintain such large military fleets if not for aggression from the others."

"I thought most of the galaxy was overrun by Floppsies," Kelly retorted. "You said they sharpen their teeth chewing on planets and go sunbathing in photospheres of stars."

"I never said either of those things," Libby admonished the ambassador. "I'm beginning to think you get your scientific facts from your son, who has a very active imagination for a nine-year old. As it happens, the Floppsies do fill a sort of a protective role for the species in the sections of the galaxy they control. They simply don't allow outsiders into their space."

"Why are you so sure the Cayl Empire species would be better off with the tunnel network rather than opening up their wallets and taking care of their own affairs?"

"Because none of them are the Cayl. Rather than my going into detail and ruining your first impression, why don't you wait until you get a chance to talk with them next month? Besides, there's a young man entering the office and Donna has already gone home."

"Who is he?" Kelly asked, as she pushed her chair back and rose to her feet.

"Press."

The ambassador fantasized for a moment about locking her office door and playing possum until the reporter gave up and left. When Chastity had launched her galactic news service for humans three years earlier, the ambassador had been the very first subscriber. It wasn't until the freshly-minted reporters began showing up at the embassy every day that she realized how the news is made. Reluctantly, she waved her door open and called, "Come in."

"Bob Steelforth, Galactic Free Press. Thank you for seeing me, Mrs. Ambassador."

"I'm afraid I don't have much time to give you, Bob. It's my turn to cook Friday dinner."

"That's alright," the young reporter told her generously. "I just have a few questions about the sovereign communities conference."

"Before you ask, you should know that Daniel Cohan, our junior consul, is handling the pre-conference negotiations."

"Great. How do you spell that name?"

"He spells it C-O-H-A-N," Kelly replied.

"Let's see," Bob mumbled, tapping away on his tab. "Who? – Daniel Cohan. What? – Third Annual Conference of Sovereign Human Communities. When? – 8:30 AM Local Human Time, Cycle 3.25. Where? – Empire Convention Center, Union Station. Why?" He paused here and looked expectantly at Kelly.

"Why what?"

"Huh? I already have 'what'. 'Why' is the next screen on my reporter tab. See?"

Kelly took the proffered tab and read the screen heading out loud. "How to write effective news stories."

"My editor says I have to use this until it becomes second nature," the young reporter admitted.

Kelly sighed. She'd suspected for some time that the Union Station editor of the Galactic Free Press had been taking advantage of her good nature to break in cub reporters, but this was getting ridiculous.

"Is this your first assignment, Bob?"

"For the Galactic Free Press it is. They hired me because I had four years of experience on the Humans desk for the Grenouthians, but this is completely different. The bunnies didn't think anything we did was important enough for interviews or analysis. They just wanted a lot of immersive video of disasters and crimes of passion. I couldn't take it anymore."

"Good for you," Kelly said, warming to the young reporter. "Half of my job is trying to convince aliens that we're not the species the Grenouthians make us out to be. So, do you want to know why Daniel is in charge of the conference, or why the conference is taking place?"

"Uh, why the conference is taking place," Bob replied. After a moment's hesitation, he added, "The editor told me that I should get a quote if possible. On the record."

"This will be the third conference of sovereign human communities hosted on Union Station," Kelly said, starting at the beginning for the young man. "The original participants came from recently established colonies on relatively local terraformed worlds belonging to the Dollnicks and the Drazens, and there was a delegation from a human academy on a Verlock world as well. The second year,

Junior Consul Cohan reached out to human communities on open worlds throughout the tunnel network. Nearly two hundred local governments participated, though many of those represented different communities from the same worlds."

"Why the conference? What are they trying to accomplish?"

"The main attraction at present is establishing commercial ties with one another and looking for ways to reduce overhead costs through sharing resources. For example, CoSHC already leases a Stryxnet connection for member use, which is cheaper than renting bandwidth from the species whose planets they're living on."

"CoSHC is the Conference of Sovereign Human Communities?"

"Exactly," Kelly said. "We use a lot of acronyms in diplomacy."

"And what's the embassy's interest in sponsoring the conference? I thought EarthCent was set up to deal with aliens, not humans."

"That's a good question, though after thirty years of working for EarthCent, I sometimes think the humans I meet are the aliens," Kelly said with a smile. "The embassy is really just a facilitator for the conference. Daniel attends as an observer, and his job, from EarthCent's perspective, is simply making sure that the sovereign human communities don't drift so far out of Earth's sphere of influence that we become strangers to one another. I really have to head home now, but you're welcome to walk with me."

"I'll do that," Bob replied. He looked down at his tab to check that the voice-to-text function had properly taken in Kelly's speech and put the words in the right box. "Let me see, just one more question."

"How?" Kelly guessed.

"How does Junior Consul Cohan get these communities to spend the money to send representatives all the way to Union Station?" Bob asked. "I visited quite a few open worlds while working for the Grenouthians, mainly to report on crop failures, mining accidents and natural disasters. Open worlds are a new thing, at least as far as humans are concerned, and while they're building rapidly, money is usually scarce."

"Off the record," Kelly said.

"If it's off the record, how can I fill in the space on my tab?" Bob asked plaintively, displaying the "How" box to the ambassador.

"Anonymous sources say," Kelly suggested. "Unnamed officials, senior diplomatic personnel. Anything like that."

"Oh, I get it. So who pays?"

"EarthCent Intelligence. I'm pretty sure they make the money back by selling market information to the attendees, and they're probably recruiting agents on the sly as well."

"But their office is right across the corridor from us," Bob said in surprise. "My editor, Mr. Dunkirk, used to work for them. I even heard that our publisher is from the same family as the people running the intelligence agency."

"So you can stop in and ask for yourself," Kelly told him. "Think of it as investigative reporting."

Two

"Did you see the headline in this morning's paper?" Shaina asked her husband at breakfast. Many of the local humans had been caught up in Chastity's enthusiasm for the old newspaper business and adopted the archaic terminology, despite the fact that the Galactic Free Press wasn't printed on paper. It was delivered over the Stryxnet to anything that could show text and graphics, including implants with holographic heads-up displays.

"You know I never read the paper before going into the office," Daniel replied. "It's all work related, so I wait until I'm on the clock."

"But you're a salaried employee," Shaina pointed out. "There is no clock."

"It's the thought that counts. What's the lead story?"

"EarthCent Ambassador Kelly McAllister Thinks That Humans are Aliens."

"Hey, that's a good one. Walter is really developing a flair for writing headlines." The junior consul stopped to adjust his necktie, glancing at himself in the kitchen display panel that was in mirror mode. "How are he and your sister getting along these days?"

"He keeps proposing and Brinda keeps turning him down. She says that you and he are really similar in the way you separate your professional and personal lives. In Walter's case, he leaves his maturity behind at the office."

11

"What does she expect from a guy who spent his whole life in school before coming here? And as long as we're pointing out similarities, it seems that you and your sister both have a thing for younger men." He held up his hands in mock surrender as Shaina brandished a piece of pastry in a threatening manner. "Watch the suit. The press is going to be at the opening and they may want to take a picture."

Shaina bit into the sticky bun, pretending that it had been her intent all along. "Eat something," she told her husband. "You don't want to go on Paul's new ride with an empty stomach."

"I'm late already," he said, but he still took a corn muffin and twisted off the sugar-glazed top. "Besides, I hear the ride involves magnetic levitation, so the people below me might prefer it if my stomach is empty."

"Don't be morbid. You liked the rollercoaster, didn't you?"

"Yeah, but Joe says that Paul and Jeeves really outdid themselves this time. They combined a ride with a game, and it's supposed to provide a better flying experience than the Frunge wings sets."

"I'm just glad Jeeves is keeping busy." Shaina stopped and took a sip from her coffee before continuing. "Now that we're only doing the four auctions a year, I know that he was getting pressure from the older Stryx to find something constructive to do with his time. Jeeves says they're trying to groom him to be some sort of diplomat, and I know he was gone for a few weeks on a negotiating mission. Dring pointed out that the other young Stryx who attend Libby's experimental school always leave to go traveling after a few years of close contact with human children, but Jeeves is originally from Union Station and he's attached himself to the McAllisters."

"Do you think that working in a theme park is a constructive use of time for one of the most powerful sentients the galaxy has ever known?"

"You have to remember that Jeeves isn't any older than Paul or us, even if he does have instant access to the shared memory of the Stryx and an IQ higher than you can count. Besides, the first-generation Stryx still do all of the heavy lifting. They just want to see their offspring developing in positive directions."

"I guess I can accept that," Daniel said, glancing over at their baby boy who was asleep in the bassinet next to Shaina's chair. "I'll tell everybody that you wanted to come, but when we called for an InstaSitter, all they had left were spies."

"Or reporters," Shaina added, before blowing him a goodbye kiss.

Daniel wasn't sure exactly what to tell the lift tube after he got in, but then he remembered that Joe had referred to the new attraction as the "Physics Ride," so he tried that. The capsule moved off smoothly.

"Libby?" Daniel asked out loud.

"Yes, Daniel," the station librarian responded.

"Any messages related to CoSHC this morning?"

"There were some late booth requests for the trade show which I forwarded to Donna for processing. Two of the new communities you're bringing in had questions about travel reimbursement from EarthCent Intelligence, which I sent on to Blythe. And there was a request from the Mayor of Floaters to arrange a press conference if possible. He's bringing a prototype of a two-man sports floater to the conference and they're hoping to get some free publicity, so I passed that on to Chastity."

"I'm beginning to think that Donna and her girls basically run things for the humans around here," the junior consul observed.

The lift tube capsule came to a halt and the door opened without a confirmation or denial from Libby about Daniel's hypothesis. The deck area was crowded with young humans and aliens, most of them wearing, or in the process of donning, a tight wrap-around over-garment. The unmistakable sound of a fairground organ assaulted his ears, and the white puffs of steam rising from its pipes drew his eyes. He walked over to investigate.

"Morning, Joe," Daniel yelled over the din. "Where on Earth did you find this thing?"

The owner of Mac's Bones motioned for the new arrival to step closer. When Daniel came within arm's reach of Joe, the sound faded into the distance, and the junior consul realized he had entered a personal acoustic suppression field.

"Could you repeat the question?" Joe asked.

"I wondered where on Earth you found this thing."

"Ohio. Kelly's parents have taken to antiquing in their old age. Her dad spotted this circus calliope in a barn and thought I might enjoy fixing it up. It took a year's worth of over-sized diplomatic pouches to get all the parts to us, but the Stryx were good sports about it."

"They fit the boiler in a diplomatic pouch?"

"These organs are a chore to tune, so I went modern on the boiler to make sure the steam always comes out at the same temperature. That and a few other modifications should keep it happy for weeks at a time."

"If you say so," Daniel replied, steeling himself to exit the audio suppression field. "Does it have to be so loud?"

"That's the whole point of the thing. When they played these at fairs or carnivals back on Earth, you could hear them for miles."

"Well, it's a show stopper. I see it even makes its own confetti."

"Damnation!" Joe swore, diving for the emergency kill switch. An alignment spacer had slipped out of place and the paper roll which acted as a mechanical program for the music was in the process of shredding itself. "You're in luck," the frustrated mechanic told the junior consul. "It's going to take a few hours to modify the feed so this can't happen again. Tell Paul to have Libby play something."

"Will do," Daniel said, setting off to find Paul and Jeeves in the crowd.

"Over here," Paul yelled, when he spotted Daniel. The proud co-creator of the new theme park attraction was standing on a small platform with Aisha, who carried their recently adopted girl in a baby sling. The baby wore a cute pair of pink ear protectors with a prominently displayed rating of 140 decibels over her little head.

"Hi, Aisha. Paul. Quite a crowd you've got here."

"We're almost at capacity, but I stashed a levitation suit for you," Paul said. "Are you ready for the ride of your life?"

"How come you aren't suiting up?" Daniel asked, accepting the proffered bundle from Paul. "Do I put these on right over my clothes?" he continued, without waiting for an answer to his first question.

"Just pull the flaps over and the magnets will seal everything tight," Paul said. "There's a towel on the belt if you need it. I'm not flying today because I'm in charge."

"I'm not afraid of flying," Samuel announced, appearing at Daniel's elbow. "Banger flies all of the time, and he says that it's just like riding a bicycle."

"Have you ever ridden a bicycle?" Daniel inquired.

"Of course," the boy replied. "Grandma sent me one."

"In the diplomatic pouch," Aisha added, answering the junior consul's unasked question. "Shaina must have stayed home with your baby and I don't blame her. I would never have brought Fenna if Paul hadn't found her these cute ear protectors."

"I'm surprised anything short of a suppression field can keep out the sound of those steam whistles."

"The ear muffs are just a fashion statement," Paul explained. "That volume of sound would go right through a baby's skull without a suppression field, so I put a miniature Dollnick generator in the headset. Speaking of which, Joe must have ripped another roll or we'd be yelling to make ourselves heard right now."

"I know it's a theme park and all, but does it have to be that loud?" Daniel asked. He finished securing his leggings and moved on to the long-sleeved top. "And Joe said it's going to be a while to fix whatever went wrong, so you'd better have Libby play something over the station system."

"The music was actually Dorothy and Mist's idea," Paul told the junior consul. "We had them invite some of their friends to serve as beta-testers last week, and we ended up with hundreds of teenagers flying around in here. The girls asked Libby to pipe in some music because they said it was like watching an immersive without the sound. It hadn't occurred to me that magnetic suspension fields would make the ride so silent, other than the screaming, of course."

"Well, I'm as ready as I ever will be," Daniel said, flexing his arms in the garment.

"Pull it all tight," Paul instructed him. "You want the suit to act as a second skin. And put on the helmet. It's not just to shield your eyes from spatters and to protect your head from accidental kicks. It also neutralizes the weight of your head."

"So your neck doesn't get tired," Samuel added.

Daniel hesitated a moment, helmet in hand. "I get the bit about accidental kicking or a poke in the eye, but what kind of spatters are we talking about here?"

"That's from the game part," Paul told him. "Swimming around in the air is fun, and we've got the magnetic fields all tuned so it doesn't feel that different from being in a pool or an ocean, but that's not enough to keep kids coming back. I'm going to start bringing up the power now."

"It's great exercise," Aisha told the junior consul. "I've been stopping in and swimming for a half-hour before going to the studio. Libby has already agreed to set aside two hours in the early morning on the human clock for grown-ups who just want to fly laps without getting shot at."

"Shot at?" Daniel suddenly felt light-headed, and then he realized his feet had drifted up off the deck and he was beginning to turn a slow somersault. Samuel flew a small circle around him, doing a modified version of the breaststroke that his father had taught him a few years earlier on the wastewater treatment deck.

"Put your helmet on," Paul yelled, just as the deck came alive with the recorded sounds of a calliope from Libby's library.

17

Daniel pulled on his helmet, which didn't do enough to cut down on the blaring carnival music. Then he stretched out his arms and legs like a skydiver, which had the effect of stopping his slow rotation. The feeling was very much like swimming in water, with none of the queasiness associated with weightlessness. The magnetic fields that held him suspended by attracting and repulsing the Verlock-manufactured monopoles threaded into the fabric of the levitation suit supplied both buoyancy and resistance.

Samuel swam right up to the junior consul and went helmet to helmet for acoustic contact. "Where's your basket?" he asked.

"My what?"

Samuel shook his head in pity and let Daniel examine the device that was tethered to the boy's wrist by a short cord. It looked like a scoop with a button on the handle, except the mouth was shaped more like a funnel than a can. Oddly enough, there were colored streaks on the inside of the scoop, like the boy had dripped paint into it or something.

A voice that Daniel immediately identified as belonging to Jeeves sounded through speakers integrated in the helmet. "Is everybody ready for the Physics Ride?"

Thousands of voices, the vast majority of them a good decade younger than the junior consul, shouted "Yes."

Everybody in the crowd who had donned a levitation suit was now swimming through the air around Daniel, making him feel like a member of an undisciplined school of fish. Dispersed through three dimensions, the section of the deck set aside for the ride felt less crowded than it had been when they were all standing on their feet. The young human faces visible behind the face shields were full of

18

anticipation. He couldn't tell what the Dollnicks or the Frunge were feeling, though he spotted a Drazen holding an extra basket with his tentacle.

"First round, warm-ups," Jeeves announced. "Five points for a catch. Ten points for a return."

Daniel checked the standard information channel on his implant but there weren't any instructions. He realized he must have missed a presentation on the rules by arriving so late, and perhaps there had even been a demonstration. He looked down and saw an unfortunate young woman who had only gotten as far as sealing one side of her leggings when the power came on. That leg was straight up in the air, like she was doing a high-kick, while she struggled to get the rest of the flying suit wrapped around her body.

"Uh, Libby?" the junior consul subvoced.

"Yes, Daniel," the Stryx librarian replied.

"You wouldn't know the rules of this game, would you?"

"Jeeves and Paul are still making them up, but I believe you're just starting a warm-up round. The goal is to catch the incoming projectiles and to shoot them back at the appropriate color-coded targets. You have to pay attention to the color as you make the catch because you can't see it once the ball is in the basket."

"I didn't get a basket."

"Oh dear, that could be awkward. I suppose you could try catching with your hands, but it's likely to be messy."

A brightly colored sphere about the size of a marble zipped past Daniel's face shield, and he turned his head to see Samuel catch it in his basket.

"Five points," the boy mouthed, and then he pointed the open end of the basket at something over the junior

19

consul's shoulder and pressed the button on the handle. Daniel twisted his head to watch as the paintball shot the gap between two more flying bodies and splattered on a moving red target disc. "Ten points."

Daniel saw a blue ball coming towards him in a lazy trajectory and tried to contort his body so it would miss, but it shattered on his chest. The paint stuck to the levitation suit rather than spraying all over the place, which he supposed was necessary to prevent the air space from turning into a cloud of colored droplets.

"What happens after the warm-ups?" he subvoced.

"In their beta-testing, the second round involved shooting at other flyers after the catch. They were talking about doing something with teams as well. I could play back the instructions Jeeves gave the people who arrived on time, but if you don't pay more attention to what's happening, you'll be declared a casualty and your suit will put you down."

"So each suit can be controlled remotely?" He tried a dolphin-style kick to work his way towards the center of the mob where he'd be out of the path of the paintballs, wherever they were coming from.

"Yes. All of the pieces you're wearing include transceivers to track the scoring and to allow Jeeves to override bad maneuvering decisions. You wouldn't want a child running head-on into a speeding adult."

"How can anybody speed in this stuff? It's sort of like being underwater, or maybe something a little less dense."

"You're not wearing the booties either?"

Daniel looked around again and saw that the other players all had plastic over their shoes. Then he noticed that some of them were moving pretty quickly without making swimming motions, as if something was thrusting them forward.

"I guess they were out of booties," he subvoced. "I really didn't know it was going to be this crowded. I thought there would be a ribbon cutting and maybe a local reporter."

"Incoming," Libby said.

"What?" Daniel looked to one side and then the other. It hadn't occurred to him that the paintballs which the players on the edges of the crowd didn't catch would keep on traveling until they hit something. He had foolishly looked for safety in the center of the play space, but now he was alone and projectiles were coming in from every direction. He squirmed and twisted like a fish on a hook, but before he could find a Dollnick to hide behind, a little red light began blinking on the helmet's visor. The levitation suit stopped responding and lowered him to the floor.

Kelly was wandering around the deck below to watch Samuel, and she greeted her junior consul loudly as soon as he removed his helmet. "You look like a Jackson Pollock. Maybe you're getting too old for this sort of thing."

"I didn't get a basket," Daniel shouted back. "Or the booties."

Kelly shook her head to show she hadn't understood and led the junior consul over to the calliope, where Joe had his upper body in the guts of the machine. She unclipped something from his belt and the canned carnival sounds faded into the distance. "At least now we won't have to shout," the ambassador said. "Anything new with your conference?"

"Nothing Donna and the girls can't handle. Oh, wait. I thought it would be a good idea to have a keynote speaker this year, and the delegates who took the time to fill out my questionnaire agreed. The thing is, they all wanted to give the honor to the ambassador from their host species."

"You mean the consortium world communities wanted the Drazen ambassador, the terraformed world communities wanted the Dollnick ambassador and the academies wanted a Verlock?"

"Yes. The back-and-forth was getting a bit contentious, so I suggested you as a compromise."

"That's sweet of you, Daniel, but I'm going to be very busy preparing for the Stryx open house."

"Too late," the junior consul informed his boss. "They already voted and you're it."

Three

"Wow! You've got so much cool stuff. I wish Metoo was here to see it all." Dorothy gazed in awe at the ceiling-high row of deep shelves packed with a crazy array of every object imaginable. Most of it was obviously of alien manufacture, but beneath the counter, which ran the whole breadth of the gigantic room, she spotted some human-style luggage, sporting gear, and a pair of umbrellas, which was especially strange since it didn't rain on Stryx stations.

"It's not our stuff, or at least, we don't think of it that way," Libby replied. "The purpose of a lost-and-found is to return lost items to their rightful owners, although that isn't always possible for temporal and spatial reasons. Your job is to help anybody who comes looking for something they've lost, and to catalog items the maintenance bots bring in if nobody claims them."

"I understand, and I really appreciate that you hired me," Dorothy replied, rummaging through the closest shelf. Unlike her mother, she never felt the urge to look at the ceiling while talking to the station librarian. "Just give me a little time and I bet I'll get the whole place cleaned out."

"That's very ambitious of you, Dorothy, but I should explain that most of the owners are long since deceased.

And you are only looking at the first row of shelves. This storeroom is approximately the same size as Mac's Bones."

"Oh," the sixteen-year-old said, her mouth gaping. "Then there must be a gazillion things in here."

"I really wish that Jeeves had never introduced that term to my students. It's very imprecise. This particular lost-and-found is for items abandoned on the nitrogen/oxygen decks of the station, and the bots bring in a few hundred items a day."

"So you're adding a little over a hundred thousand pieces a year," Dorothy estimated. "That's at least a million items a decade, or more than ten million a century. Since Gryph built the station over fifty million years ago, I'd say it's got to be near a gazillion by now."

"If your initial assumptions were correct, the number would be five trillion, but you made three mistakes. Can you tell me what they are?"

"But I graduated already," Dorothy complained. "Do you still quiz Blythe and Chastity like they never left school?"

"Yes," her former teacher replied.

"Oh. Then I guess I shouldn't have started by assuming that a few hundred items a day was three hundred."

"Correct."

"And I forgot that some people might come looking for their lost stuff, so the number could actually be a little less."

"I'll give you partial credit."

"Why partial credit?"

"We're able to figure out from our station imaging who owns most of the items left behind by visitors, and in those cases, we contact them and arrange for delivery," Libby explained. "For example, we get lots of luggage forgotten in restaurants or bathrooms by travelers who are waiting for connections between ships. By the time they realize they've left something behind they're light-years away, but as long as we can identify the owner we'll send their luggage after them."

"Doesn't that get expensive?"

"Most ships coming through the station will accept lost luggage deliveries for their destinations as a common courtesy, though many of the lost pieces are of such low value that the owners we contact tell us to dispose of them. There's also the fact that the maintenance bots can have difficulty differentiating between lost objects and litter, and truthfully, some items may only have temporary value in the eyes of their owners."

"Like what?"

"Take a look in the blue bin under the counter."

Dorothy pulled out the blue bin and saw that it was full of silvery jewelry. On further examination, it became apparent that all of the rings and bracelets were made out of foil, probably from food wrappers or some other dis-posable packaging material. Some of it was pretty elaborate, including long, flexible chains.

"This is all throw-away stuff that people make while they're waiting for a connection," she declared confidently.

"Are you sure that the sentients who created those pieces would feel the same way?"

"They wouldn't have left them behind otherwise."

"Maybe so," Libby replied with a sigh. "But the maintenance bots tend to assume that anything shiny is of value, and we don't like to discourage their initiative just because they aren't sentient. Have you figured out your third erroneous assumption?"

"Can I have a hint?"

"Ka-ching."

"You don't keep it all forever," Dorothy exclaimed. "Of course, that would just be silly. So how often do you sell everything?"

"The shelving units you see run on a track system which snakes back and forth, leaving enough space between the rows to get in and retrieve items. From the end of the back row, the shelves travel up the side of the hold and enter the front row again. When all of the shelves in the back row are full, we open that side of the room and invite the second-hand dealers to come and bid on lots from the exposed row. The last sale was twenty-three years ago."

"How many, uh, customers come into the lost-and-found each day looking for things on the shelves?"

"The vast majority of the lost items that come in are from travelers. You might see a dozen walk-ins during a busy shift, depending on the way the clocks used by the various species are overlapping that day. Other shifts, you might be here five hours and not see a soul."

"That'll be great once my course work for the Open University picks up," Dorothy said enthusiastically. "Hey. Is that why Paul called this a 'work-study' job?"

"Yes. When Paul was an Open University student, he was employed by the lost-and-found until he started doing his own lab work."

"So how do I catalog stuff the bots bring in?"

"Flazint will be staying late today to show you the system. When I asked her to work overtime, she requested a short break to get her hair misted. Ah, here she comes now."

For a brief moment, Dorothy thought that a large bird of prey had entered the lost-and-found, but then she realized that it was an elaborate upswept hairdo of the sort favored by young Frunge women. She marveled that Flazint could walk through doors without damaging the trellis work that provided a template for her hair vines.

"Hi. I'm Flazint."

"I'm Dorothy. I love your hair. How do you keep from breaking it?"

"Practice," Flazint replied. "You start with a flexible training-trellis, so even if you run into stuff, the worst that can happen is a few split vines. I usually don't come to work like this, but it's the start of pollination season and it's the first year that my ancestors are letting me date."

"Cool. Libby was just telling me how most of the lost stuff gets found before we catalog it, but she said you'd show me what to do. I feel bad about making you stay late, though."

"I'm happy to get the overtime. I'm saving to move out with friends, but don't tell anybody," Flazint added hastily. She eyed the human girl closely, wondering if her confidence might be misplaced.

"I won't," Dorothy promised, pressing a fist to her forehead. It was a gesture she'd seen the little Frunge children on Aisha's show make when they were promising to be good, and it seemed to satisfy Flazint.

"Let's get started then. The first step is to separate the legitimate lost items from the litter," the Frunge girl explained. "All of the new stuff goes in the marked bins under the counter at this end. The borderline cases, like the foil jewelry, we keep for a little less than nine days before recycling."

"A little less than nine days?"

"A Verlock boy who worked here like a couple million years ago came up with the system, so it's all based on their calendar period of a Klunk. Whenever you come to work, you should take a few minutes to familiarize yourself with the new items in the bins under the counter at the intake end. The bins are sitting on a continuous belt that ages them towards the cold-storage end of the counter, a journey that takes one Klunk. The bots will then remove anything in blue bins for recycling, and whoever is working the counter is responsible for cataloging the unclaimed items in the white bins."

"Is there anything in the white bins now?" Dorothy left the Frunge girl behind as she ran down the length of the counter, so enthusiastic was she to get to work. "Is this one ready?"

"Well, normally you wouldn't pull it off until the bots take the blue one that's ahead of it, but I guess we can make an exception for training purposes," the girl called back. She was taking her time moving down the counter because she had to walk with her head turned sideways, so as not to catch one of her hairdo's wings on the shelves.

"Great!" Dorothy slid out the heavy white bin and heaved it onto the counter. "Wow. Is that a real gun?"

"Don't squeeze the—don't fire it again. Just put it down on the counter. The maintenance bots are supposed to report abandoned weapons immediately, but the non-lethal varieties don't count."

"Did I break anything?" Dorothy asked, more embarrassed than frightened by the accidental discharge. Other than the "Vrrriiippth" sound it had made, there was no sign that the gun had fired.

"It's alright. That's a disposable Dollnick stun pistol. They're popular with traders who want protection but don't want to hurt anybody. We get them all the time because there's no resale market for used ones, and traders

28

who buy something better or decide they don't need one anymore just leave them wherever. Press the little yellow stud on the side of the barrel. There, it's on safety now."

"So how do I catalog it? Are there tags to fill out or something?"

"First everything gets holo-imaged. See the easy-round at the end of the counter?"

"Easy-round? I don't think my implant got that right," Dorothy said.

"You know, for throwing round clay vessels," the girl explained. "I thought all the biologicals had them."

"You mean a potter's wheel? That's a big one."

"Just put the stunner on there and give it a gentle spin."

Dorothy gingerly placed the Dollnick weapon on the turntable and used her forefinger to impart a rotational force.

"Dollnick stun pistol, model 625 A, Rev L2," an artificial voice intoned. "Ready for storage."

"Now take it and find a place for it on the shelves directly behind you," Flazint said. She carefully hopped up to sit on the counter, keeping the wings of her hairdo parallel to the shelves. "The metal plate on the floor in front of each shelving unit is a lift pad, so if there isn't enough space on the shelves you can reach, just tell it to raise you up. It activates a three-sided restraining field so you can't fall off."

"No, I can fit it in here," Dorothy said. She crouched and placed the Dollnick weapon in the hollow space of what was either a floatation device from an ocean-going vessel or some sort of giant Frisbee. "Is that it?"

"Now you read the shelf number out loud for the cataloging agent to record."

"It's in Frunge," Dorothy complained.

"Just tell it you want Humanese."

"English, please," Dorothy said to the shelving unit. The active display markings on the edge of the shelf where she'd placed the gun changed into a series of letters and numbers. The closest designation to the lifesaver was JER 29/13, so she spoke the code out loud.

The cataloging system's voice confirmed the location with a verbose recitation. "Dollnick stun pistol, model 625 A, Rev L2, stored at location JER 29/13."

"So if somebody comes in looking for an item that was lost a long time ago, we get the description and the lost-and-found catalog tells us where to look?" Dorothy asked.

"Maybe once a cycle a visitor to the station comes by to check if they lost something here years ago, but for most transients, it's just the stuff under the counter," the Frunge girl told her. "But remember, the Stryx don't notify station residents when they leave stuff lying around because they don't want to turn the bots into a free maid service. So most of the walk-in traffic we get is the people who live here stopping in to see if something they lost has turned up."

"I think I could fit more stuff on these shelves if I just rearranged things a bit."

"You can't start rearranging unless you want to clean off the whole shelf, re-holo all of the items to take them out of inventory, and then reenter them all again. If you ever get to start with an empty shelving unit, begin at the bottom and pack the shelves as tightly as you can without hiding stuff. So you can't put small things behind big things, or pack items in an empty suitcase. You'll get the hang of it."

"So the shelving units are moving the opposite direction of the belt under the counter," Dorothy surmised.

"That way, the last few months of stuff is always right here at the front."

"Yup, except it takes at least twenty years to fill each row of shelves. And that's pretty much the whole job," Flazint concluded. "Go ahead and try another one."

Dorothy pulled out a surprisingly heavy object that resembled a rough file, with a handle made from two pieces of steel that were sprung apart at the end, forming a gap. The bent steel ends on either side of the gap featured a sharpened edge, one of which had a half-round cutout.

"Any idea what this is?" she asked the Frunge girl.

"It's a manicure tool of some sort," Flazint replied. "We get lots of them in here. I'm not sure about the species, though. Something with pretty big claws, I'd guess."

Dorothy placed it on the holo-platform and gave it a spin.

"Huktra talon clipper and file," the voice identified the tool.

"What's the grossest thing you ever found?" Dorothy asked her mentor, as she searched for a place to store the talon clipper on a shelf.

"Medical stuff," the other girl replied without hesitation. "There are plenty of jars with body parts on the shelves, embryos in portable stasis fields, vat-grown replacement organs that got lost along the way. Nobody ever seems to claim those, so it might all be black market."

"Is there any way to figure out where the bots found the stuff?"

"Sure, it's part of the permanent record. The bots image everything they find before they pick it up, and it all gets correlated by the storage system. Take something off the shelf and ask about it."

Dorothy pulled out the object next to where she had just stored the talon clippers and found it was a short tube with a small, round can on one side. The can had a handle on it, like a pepper-mill or a coffee grinder, and there was a little hollow sphere snugged up to one end of the tube.

"Any ideas?" she asked the Frunge girl.

"I think it's a Vergallian fishing pole. Look for a button on the side, but don't point it at me."

Dorothy quickly found a small sliding switch on the side of the tube and pushed it forward. The tube leapt in her hand, the end telescoping out to twice her height, the fishing bob dangling at the tip.

"Hey, they run the line inside the pole. My dad might like one of these."

"I hope we can figure out how to collapse it again because it will never fit on the shelf that way," Flazint said.

Dorothy pulled the slide switch back, but nothing happened.

"No luck. Maybe the tip needs to be pushed in." She carefully brought the tip of the rod down behind the counter and pressed the end against the bulkhead. Instead of retracting, the rod bent when she pushed. Dorothy stepped back, and to her relief, it returned to being a straight pole.

"Were you holding the button while you did that?"

"Yeah. Maybe the battery is dead," Dorothy speculated. "Libby? How can I make this fishing pole retract?"

"Hold the button and reel in the line," the Stryx librarian replied. "It may feel a little tight, but the bob is compressing a permanent spring. Don't worry about the line snapping.

As Dorothy gingerly reeled in the bob, a handsome Vergallian wearing rubber boots strode up to the counter.

"Be careful with that," he ordered peremptorily. "I paid fourteen hundred creds for that pole, and I just spent two weeks during the Ferlock run on Thuri Minor twiddling my thumbs."

Dorothy flushed and began to mumble an excuse, but the Frunge girl was having none of it.

"Who spends fourteen hundred creds on a fishing pole and then loses it right before vacation? Anyway, for all we know, you came in here looking for something else and you just decided to upgrade. Do you know where you lost it?"

The Vergallian glowered at the girls as he considered giving them a piece of his mind, but he was so relieved to find that the pole hadn't been stolen he decided to play along.

"Sure. I know I had it in the departure lounge for the luxury liner to Thuri Minor because I took it out of my bag to admire it. I'd bought it specifically for the vacation, you see." He furrowed his brows in concentration. "We had some time before boarding, and I remember that I went to buy some snacks. All I can think is that I must have left it at the kiosk because I needed both hands to carry back the tray.

"Where was the fishing pole stored at JER 16/16 found?" Dorothy asked the cataloging system.

"Vergallian Ferlock Pro, Deluxe Model, discovered under Star Ways departure lounge seat on..."

"That's enough," Dorothy cut off the voice. "The owner is reclaiming the fishing pole, and the talon clipper is stored at JER 16/16 now."

"Huktra talon clipper and file, stored at location JER 16/16," the cataloging system's voice acknowledged.

"Thanks," the Vergallian said. He accepted the fully retracted pole from Dorothy and turned to go. Then he remembered his manners and slapped a five-cred coin on the counter as a tip.

"You should take that," Dorothy told the Frunge girl. "I'm just in training."

"If you're sure," Flazint replied, picking up the coin. She turned her head a little and watched the Vergallian exiting the room. "He lost it less than two Klunks ago, right? Want to see something funny?"

"Sure," Dorothy replied, wondering what the Frunge girl might have in mind.

"Librarian. Does security imaging for the Star Ways departure lounge where the item from JER 16/16 was lost include footage of how the pole got under the seat?"

"Affirmative," Libby replied.

A hologram sprang to life over the turntable. It showed the bustling departure lounge, zooming in on a handsome Vergallian, who had one arm around a beautiful woman as he admired his Ferlock Pro rod. After a few minutes of this, he opened a piece of luggage and wrapped the collapsed rod tenderly in what appeared to be a woman's nightgown. The hologram caught a look of fury flashing across the woman's face, which then took on an expression of intense concentration. She said something to the man, who rose and headed off to a food kiosk.

As soon as his back was turned, the beautiful Vergallian woman thumbed open the bag, unwrapped the fishing rod, and then carefully refolded the nightgown, patting it gently into place. Then she stuck the Ferlock Pro under the seat. When the man returned with a couple of drinks and some salty snacks, she was all smiles.

"How did she get away with that?" Dorothy asked the Frunge girl.

"Didn't you see when she got all focused there for a couple of seconds?" Flazint asked. "She was zapping him with pheromones. She must have wiped out the last minute of his memory so he wouldn't remember packing the rod and then sent him for snacks. High-caste Vergallian women are scary."

Four

"So I'm supposed to find host families amongst the Union Station ambassadors for the visiting diplomats?" Kelly asked.

"Just the top emissaries," Libby reassured her. "The guests from the member worlds of the Cayl Empire who take advantage of the temporary tunnel will eventually number in the hundreds of thousands. Most of those will be from the local ruling classes, and they may prefer sleeping on their luxury ships to staying at the best hotels that can meet their physiological requirements. But it's been our experience over the years that getting the important diplomatic representatives to live quietly with an unrelated species on the station for a couple of weeks before the open house officially begins can make all of the difference in the outcome. While the temporary tunnel is open to bring the emissaries here, we'll send a sort of an exchange delegation in the opposite direction."

"Well, I'll try my best, but arranging confidential sleepovers for advanced aliens who rule star systems isn't something I do every day. We could put a few up in Mac's Bones, of course, maybe the whole bunch if they have small enough ships to park in the campgrounds."

"The idea is to get as many tunnel species involved as possible. Even if it was practical for you to provide lodging for all of the emissaries, it would be tantamount to putting all of our eggs in one basket, not to mention arousing the jealousy of the other ambassadors who already have issues with EarthCent."

"So I need to convince the least friendly ambassadors from the Naturals League to host an alien emissary from the Cayl Empire?"

"I knew you'd agree," Libby said, choosing to ignore the question in Kelly's tone. "I have a presentation on the emissaries ready to show you, but I thought you might want to bring in some of your support staff."

"Donna for sure, and she should be arriving at any minute. Daniel has enough to do getting ready for CoSHC, but I'd want to get somebody from EarthCent Intelligence in here. Maybe Chastity as well, since her paper will be covering the event."

"Do you want me to contact them and see if they're available now?"

"Yes, please," Kelly replied. "Is there a precedent for calling a meeting with the other ambassadors for the sake of discussing who is willing to put up a visiting emissary?"

"Such a meeting takes place every open house, though none of the current ambassadors were present the last time we had one on Union Station. If you'd like, I'll contact the ambassadors whose living quarters offer a potential match for our guests and arrange for a meeting."

"That will be a great help. For a minute there, I thought I was going to have to go around begging."

"Begging may still be required," Libby informed her. "Donna just arrived in the outer office, and Chastity and Clive are on their way. Chastity was just wrapping up her morning practice with Marcus, and I caught Clive as he was dropping the twins off at my school."

"Don't you think three hours a day after school is a bit much for six-year-olds to spend practicing ballroom dancing?" Kelly blurted out the question before she could stop herself. "I know they have a lot of energy, but still…"

"As their godmother and school teacher, I admit I do monitor their sessions," Libby replied thoughtfully. "Vivian would gladly dance twice as long, but Jonah will probably quit before he turns seven. According to Jeeves, he's only stuck it out this long because he knows how much his sister enjoys it."

"They do get along well for siblings. Sometimes it goes the other way with twins."

"Knock, knock," Donna said, entering the office. "Libby told me that we're having a meeting. I put on the coffee for Chastity and Clive, and it looks like you already bought donuts."

"Donut. It was just the one and I didn't have breakfast," Kelly added defensively, crumpling the empty bag to dispose of the evidence.

"Who else is coming?"

"Clive and Chastity are it unless—hello, Thomas. Are you here for the meeting?"

"Clive pinged and asked me to come," Thomas replied. "With Lynx and Woojin checking up on the new field offices and Blythe only working part-time, I'm sort of number two in the organization."

"Two and a half," Kelly corrected him.

"Anyway, Herl was on the station last night and we had a meeting about the Cayl Empire," Thomas said. "It turns out that the Grenouthians sent a documentary crew to visit the Cayl less than ten thousand years ago, so I spent the whole night watching the episodes that Libby dug up for me. It seems that one of the species, the Shuga, once went

38

so far as to purpose-build artificial people to act as their ruling class. Could you imagine humans ever doing such a thing?"

"Not really, no," Kelly said. "Besides, as long as we're part of the tunnel network, it wouldn't make sense. As soon as the Stryx recognized our purpose-built leaders as sentient, they could walk away and find something more interesting to do than supervising humans. Wouldn't you?"

"I hadn't thought of that," Thomas admitted.

"Libby?" Donna asked. "Are there any Shugas coming to the open house?"

"They accepted the invitation, and one of the emissaries will be a Shuga," the station librarian replied. "Clive and Chastity are entering the outer office."

"Bring your own chairs," Kelly hollered towards her open door.

"Nothing like a Monday morning meeting," Clive said, entering Kelly's office with a chair in each hand. "Did you do a sweep, Thomas?"

"As soon as I came in," the artificial person replied, waggling his little finger. "This built-in sniffer is worth every cred."

"Hi, all," Chastity greeted them, entering the room immediately after Clive. "Thanks for inviting me. Shall I assume this is on deep background?"

"Yes," Kelly replied. "Strictly off the record. I know that you'll be covering the open house once it officially begins whether the Stryx invite the press or not, but I'd prefer to coordinate ahead of time so we can avoid the problems we ran into at the last CoSHC conference."

"I created an employee handbook to specifically prohibit a repeat of that behavior," Chastity replied. "I admit it was totally unprofessional, and the only thing I can say in our defense is that the reporter in question was employed by EarthCent Intelligence for two years before we hired him away."

"I train them to take lots of pictures," Thomas interjected modestly.

"I understand, and I appreciate that you didn't publish any of those images, Chastity," Kelly said. "In this case, a Stryx open house is new for all of us, so there will be plenty of room for mistakes. Libby has prepared a presentation to give us an idea of what to expect from the primary species. Also, I just learned that one of my duties as hostess is to find families in the diplomatic community willing to invite an alien emissary to live with them for a quiet get-acquainted."

"That should be interesting," Donna commented dryly.

"Libby? Do you want to start now?" Kelly asked.

The Stryx librarian brought to life above the ambassador's display desk a three-dimensional map showing the Cayl Empire. "I've adjusted the sizes of the stars and the distances between them for the sake of illustration," Libby said, getting right down to business. "You'll notice that the Cayl expanded their holdings in a controlled manner, so they rule a roughly spherical volume of space with their home system at the center. In recent millennia, they've been turning down invitations to conquer bordering species, in some cases even ignoring military provocations because they didn't want to overextend their interior lines of supply and communications."

"Smart," Clive said. "No point fighting wars so far from home that you can't defend what you take without spending a fortune."

"I'm only showing the stars with occupied planets in this hologram, and I've colored them according to the four main factions within the empire. While the Cayl are in control of military defense and certain judicial functions, the day-to-day life in their empire is dominated by four advanced species and their followers. The stars I'm pulsing red now are under the economic control of the Shuga, whom Thomas was talking about just a few minutes ago."

"What do they look like?" Chastity interrupted.

A silver-skinned creature with a crest of feathers replaced the map. The hologram began rotating slowly, showing two arms and two legs, though the neck was about twice as long as one would have expected given the other proportions. There was a large lump in the Shuga's belly that made it look like the creature had swallowed a cantaloupe.

"Is it pregnant?" Chastity asked.

"Incubating an egg," the station librarian replied. "The males and females both have an external pouch for carrying eggs and keeping them warm, and they share the incubation duties after the female lays the egg."

"So they might be comfortable with the Fillinducks, since they're egg layers, or with the Grenouthians, since they have pouches," Kelly ventured. "Who's next?"

The Shuga was replaced by the holographic map, and a section of blue stars now pulsed alongside the red.

"Is it my imagination or are the blue star systems and red star systems basically alternating?" Clive asked.

"Precisely," Libby replied. "I'll add the others since you've already spotted the pattern."

An approximately equivalent number of green and yellow stars began pulsing, and it became obvious to everyone that although each of the factions controlled

41

about the same number of systems, they were all mixed together, as if the empire had been stirred in three dimensions to create an even distribution.

"So the Cayl kept their subjects weak by not allowing any of them to control contiguous blocks of space," Kelly surmised.

"Not weak, but diffused," Libby replied. "The absolute distance between planetary systems is mainly an economic barrier, the price of the energy involved in making faster-than-light jumps. The Cayl use their power to ensure that the factions within their empire always have economic incentives to maintain strong ties with their neighbors, rather than becoming mini-empires within a protectorate. It's proved to be a very stable system."

"Who are the other dominant species?" Chastity asked.

The map was again replaced by an alien form, this one sporting four arms and a trunk in place of a nose.

"Four arms makes it a candidate for a Dollnick sleepover, and that tentacle might put the Drazens at ease," Kelly said.

"It's a trunk if they breathe through it," Donna observed. "Tentacles are for grabbing stuff."

"He looks like Ganesh," Chastity declared. "Don't you recognize him from Aisha's collection? He's the Hindu god of something."

"So you think I should invite him to stay with us?"

"The alien you are referring to is a Nangor, and he wouldn't be comfortable in your home. The Nangors are herbivores and great gardeners, so he would find the metallic environment in Mac's Bones too sterile," Libby explained.

"Who else?" Chastity asked.

The Nangor was replaced by a figure that looked a little like an elongated turtle. The torso was definitely encased in a shell of sorts, but it didn't look like there could possibly be room inside for the creature to retract its arms and legs. The head, on the other hand, was practically neckless, and the skull was topped with small armored plates, rather than hair.

"Are they good at math?" Kelly asked. "It reminds me of the Verlocks for some reason."

"The Tzvim are indeed accomplished mathematicians," Libby replied. "Their early history was similar to that of the Tharks, a military species that nearly wiped itself out. In spite of its appearance, the Tzvim are the most peaceable and friendly of the leading Cayl Empire cultures."

"Isn't there one more dominant species?" Chastity asked.

"The Lood," Libby acknowledged. The hologram switched to a figure wearing a brilliant purple cloak edged with white fur. A full-faced golden mask hid the creature's features, but the contours appeared to be the same as a human face. The arms, legs, hands and feet all agreed with human proportions as well.

"Is there something behind the mask we shouldn't see?" Donna asked.

"The Lood are similar to the Vergallians in many ways," Libby replied. "Their ruling class can be easily distinguished from the commoners by appearance, namely the presence of the all-seeing eye." The golden mask dissolved, and the humans winced at the beautiful face marred by an eye in the middle of the forehead.

"Ugh," Donna said for them all.

"Does the third eye give them special powers?" Clive asked.

"That's the tricky part," Libby replied. "The ruling-class Lood males are capable of compelling some humanoid species to obey them, and the ruling-class women can detect falsehoods, creating a sort of balance of power. We aren't positive about whether the Loods will be able to influence or read humans because the two species have never been in contact before."

"You mean one of those guys could turn us into zombies?" Kelly demanded.

"In terms of capabilities and persistence, the effects the elite male Loods can produce are similar to what upper-class Vergallian women do with pheromones."

"You're not giving me a lot of confidence," Kelly retorted. "Do you want me to put up these mind-stealers in Mac's Bones?"

"It's up to you, of course, but I'd actually hoped you'd take in the Cayl guest."

"The Cayl?" Chastity interrupted. "I thought this whole open house was about trying to woo the species made available by the dissolution of the Cayl Empire."

"That's correct, but as long as the Cayl remain in charge, even through a temporary play-for-pay arrangement, they'll expect to be treated with the respect due to the rulers of a large empire."

"What do they look like?" Donna asked.

The hologram above the display desk was replaced by something that looked like a cross between a polar bear and a man. The face and hands were the only exposed body parts that weren't covered with fine white hair, though the oversized snout might have benefitted aesthetically from some fur. The Cayl's lips were drawn back in a smile or a grimace, showing a mouthful of teeth to rival Beowulf's. Stubby black claws sprouted from the backs of the hands behind each finger, but something instinctive warned the humans that if the creature made a fist, those claws would protrude like daggers.

"How big is it?" Chastity asked. "Can you add Clive to the hologram for scale?"

A three-dimensional image of the Director of EarthCent Intelligence carrying two chairs appeared next to the bear. The Cayl didn't look half as threatening when it turned out to be a head shorter than Clive.

"Well, he is smiling," Kelly said, deciding to take an optimistic view of the toothy display. "Other than the claws and the teeth, he could be more cuddly than a Grenouthian. But I'll want to show my family the hologram before inviting him to stay in our home."

"I wonder if Dring has any experience with the Cayl?" Clive mused.

"It seems likely, but you'll have to ask him," Libby replied. "We know nothing of what the Makers did between the time they asked us not to see them and the time Dring took up residence in Mac's Bones."

"You'll be updating all of our implants with their languages?" Kelly asked.

"They're already included," Libby said. "The Cayl Empire has been a model of stability for millions of years, and enough young Stryx tour through their space that we can keep the translation tables up-to-date with the latest slang."

"You've been awfully quiet," Kelly said to Thomas. "Don't you have any questions?"

"I'm afraid that the documentaries I've watched have already biased my opinions," Thomas replied. "According to the Grenouthians, all of the Cayl Empire species tend to get out of hand if there aren't any Cayl around, so we should probably be prepared."

"You don't think that Gryph can handle a few hundred thousand rude tourists?" Kelly asked jokingly.

"They'll be visiting the station, not off in their own fleet like the Wanderers," Thomas said. "They all look like tough customers in their own ways, and the four species Libby just showed us are dominant in their own spheres of influence. For millions of years, they've taken their orders from the Cayl and nobody else."

"He's got a point," Clive said. "We should at least prepare an advisory for our merchants on the station so they won't be taken by surprise if Gryph cuts the aliens some extra slack."

"Are you planning on trying to cultivate intelligence sources among the open house guests?" Kelly inquired.

"We'll make an effort, but if they don't join the tunnel network after the open house, there's not much point in adding them to the payroll. We simply don't have the resources to try to keep up with every sentient in the galaxy. Even the Drazens limit their intelligence efforts to the species they come across in the regular course of business."

"What about threats we don't know about?" Chastity protested. "Humans who want to establish their own colony worlds have to go off the tunnel network to try. Aren't you supposed to be tracking the problems they might run into?"

"We can't do everything, Chas," Clive told his sister-in-law. "The Stryx will put in exits for any of the tunnel-affiliated species once a world warrants the attention, but it doesn't make any sense to do it for every settlement effort. What's the current criteria, Libby?"

"We'll provide tunnel access to a colony once it passes two-hundred million inhabitants or an investment of two trillion Stryx cred."

"Why wait so long?" Kelly asked. "Wouldn't the colonies have a much greater chance of success if they had tunnel access from the beginning?"

"It requires a great deal of energy to create and hold open a tunnel," Libby explained. "A large investment in terraforming or infrastructure shows that the species is taking the colonization effort seriously. And we will extend protection to colony worlds before they reach the scale for tunnel access, provided the space was undisputed when the colony was founded and the request is made through an ambassador for the species on one of the stations."

"I have a question," Thomas said suddenly. "Do the Cayl recognize the artificial people created by members of their empire as sentients, the way the Stryx do? If not, does that mean they can keep AI enslaved?"

"The Cayl policy on AI is currently similar to ours, which is one of the reasons we're sorry to see their empire winding down operations," Libby replied. "Some of their member species would prefer a different approach, and it may be a sticking point if negotiations get that far."

"Who's going on the exchange delegation you mentioned, Libby? Are any humans welcome?"

"We'll be sending a science ship to anchor the tunnel for the open house, and there's room for a few humans to accompany the ship and visit the Cayl homeworld. Jeeves has been in touch with the Cayl at the highest levels, and he suggested sending Woojin and Lynx, providing Clive approves. And he said something about adding Brinda in case there's an opportunity for a 'going-out-of-empire' auction."

"I think it's a great idea," Clive said. "Lynx has plenty of diplomatic experience from her cultural attaché work, and Wooj is our military expert, so he'll appreciate what the Cayl have done."

"Sounds good to me," Kelly said. "Are any Stryx going, Libby?"

"Our science ships are all constructed around a resident second-generation Stryx," the librarian replied. "Think of them as miniature versions of our stations that spend all of their time moving around and looking into things. The science ship that will be carrying Lynx and Woojin is run by Stryx Vrine."

"Banger's parent? Small galaxy."

Five

"I only need half of the Galaxy room, and only for the first morning," Daniel reiterated.

"Your reservation shows that you reserved the full amphitheatre for four human days," the unemotional Dollnick administrator of the Empire Convention Center replied. "That's twenty-six thousand creds, which includes the multi-day discount.

"Then there's been some kind of mistake," the junior consul insisted. "I made a three-day reservation for the Nebulae room for the trade show, and I went back later and added a day to the front-end, to give the vendors a chance to set up before the event."

"The only reservation I'm showing for you is the Galaxy room. The Nebulae room is no longer available on the dates you've requested. The Hortens have it reserved through the end of the cycle for a religious revival."

"I don't believe this," Daniel practically shouted. "I made these reservations three cycles ago and I have confirmations!"

"If you don't believe me, let's walk down to the Nebulae room right now and you can accept Gortunda as your savior," the Dollnick responded dryly. "I understand that the Hortens have reduced the tithing obligation to seven percent for new converts."

"Look," Daniel said, waving his tab under the towering Dollnick's nose. "Three-day reservation for the Nebulae room, deposit accepted."

"You must have cancelled and transferred the deposit to the Galaxy room," the Dollnick said. "I suggest you check with the station librarian, since she does our recordkeeping. If you want to change your reservation for the Galaxy room at this late date, there will be a six thousand cred cancellation fee, per day."

"This is ridiculous," Daniel yelled, losing his cool completely. Then he turned on his heel and stalked out of the administrator's office towards the nearest lift tube. "EarthCent Embassy," he told it on entering.

As the lift tube door slid closed and the capsule whisked him away towards the embassy, he tried to figure out what had gone wrong. Daniel remembered making the reservations and then later putting in the change request over the display desk in his small office next to Kelly's. The only explanation he could come up with was that one of the advanced species had altered his reservations through some technological trickery, perhaps a Vergallian attempt to sabotage CoSHC. He thought about contacting Clive or talking to Libby, but when he exited the lift tube, he decided to start with Donna.

"You look pretty unhappy," the embassy's office manager observed when Daniel slumped into the chair next to her desk. "Some last minute problems with the conference?"

"The convention center messed up our reservations," Daniel admitted. "I know perfectly well that I ordered the Nebulae room for three days, and half of the Galaxy amphitheatre for the first morning. At the last preconference holo-meeting, some of the attendees complained that they needed more time to set up, so I added a day to the beginning of the Nebulae room reservation. Now the convention center is saying that I reserved the whole Galaxy room for four days, and that the Nebulae room is booked solid by the Hortens to the end of the cycle. I showed the Dollnick the original confirmation on my tab, but he said I must have cancelled."

"Was it the same Dollnick who took your order?" Donna asked.

"I made the reservations on my display desk. I didn't talk to anybody."

"Hmm. Shall we ask Libby if she still has the records from your desk?"

"Knock yourself out," Daniel grunted. His mind was running a light-year a second as he tried to figure out what he was going to do with over two hundred vendors from CoSHC. The conference part of the event could take place almost anywhere with enough space, but the vendors could hardly set up booths on the steep coliseum seating of the amphitheatre.

"Libby? Can you locate all transactions from Daniel's display desk regarding the Empire Convention Center reservations for the upcoming event?"

"Three transactions located," Libby replied. "I'll display them in order, starting with the initial reservation."

"You see!" Daniel exclaimed, pointing as a ghostly image of his own hand blocked out a three-day section on the human calendar interface for the convention center's reservation system and hit the "Book it now" button.

"And here's the second transaction, which took place just a few minutes after the first," Libby said. This time, they watched Daniel's fingers squeezing a 3D representation of the Galaxy room until it transformed from a full amphitheatre to a half. Then the fingers moved to the calendar and tried shrinking a day down to a half a day, but it kept springing back. Eventually, he gave up and selected "Book it now."

"Maybe I did take it for a full day and forgot," Daniel admitted. "I remember I intended to reserve just the morning."

"And here's the third transaction, from right after your last pre-conference meeting," Libby informed them. This time the ghostly hand seemed to wander through the reservation system menus, searching for the right option. The three-day reservation for the Nebulae room finally appeared, and the fingers tried stretching it to cover the previous day without success. Daniel's other hand entered the hologram, and he appeared to be trying to hold the end date of the reservation pinched with the fingers of one hand, while pulling the start date with the fingers of the other. Instead, the reservation period lengthened in the wrong direction. Next the fingers pushed the two ends back together, squeezing the date range down to nothing as he prepared to start from scratch. The hologram seemed to glitch, and suddenly the calendar showed a one-day reservation.

"Freeze," Donna said. "Did you see that? I think you must have accidentally brought up the other reservation by gesturing with your left hand. It's dangerous to use both hands at the same time in these holo-systems. Continue."

Daniel watched in horror as he stretched the Galaxy room reservation to cover four days, and then poked the "Confirm changes," button, apparently not taking the time to read a block of small print that popped up.

"Freeze," Donna said again. "Libby? Can you zoom in on the small print?"

"Reservations for one half of the Galaxy room may not be extended beyond three human days," Daniel read out loud. "The date range you have selected will result in your order being changed to a reservation for the whole room."

"I'm afraid the Dollnick was right," Donna said.

Daniel pulled out his tab and scrolled rapidly through his correspondence until he saw the unopened change confirmation from the Empire Convention Center. He'd been so confident in his actions that he hadn't bothered reading the later confirmation when it arrived. Opening it now, he saw that the reservation was exactly as the holo-record had shown.

"I can't believe I messed this up and it's nobody's fault but my own," Daniel said angrily. "I remember now that you asked me if I had confirmations for the reservations and I told you I did. I should have just let you handle it from the start."

"Don't be so hard on yourself," Donna told him. "It was your first time using their reservation system. I've been booking rooms at the Empire for over thirty years and I still ask Libby to double-check that I get it right. It could have turned out worse, you know. You'll just have to do everything in the Galaxy room."

"The central stage isn't big enough for all the booths, and half of the delegations to this thing only come for a chance to market their products. More than half."

"So you'll have to use the floor space under the seating tiers where there's plenty of room. The delegates will probably compliment you for keeping down costs and saving them some walking."

"There's meeting space under the seating? I thought it would all be taken up by stone arches."

"The Verlocks are the only species that uses real stone for anything on the station. The Galaxy room seating is some kind of plastic stuff that looks like stone, and it's all supported by carbon fiber webbing that's hung off of the station spokes. I've been under there a number of times helping with props and scenery changes for the productions the girls were in when they were younger."

"You're serious?" Daniel felt like the weight of a Verlock amphitheatre had been lifted from his shoulders. "How's the access?"

"There are four passages to get from the stage to the galleries under the seats," Donna said, working from memory. "Visitors normally enter and exit the Galaxy room on the same deck as the convention center, which brings them into the seating area about two thirds of the way up. But half of the seats and all of the stage are really on the deck below, and you can tell the people who reserved booth space to have their stuff delivered to the lower level, so they don't have to carry it down the stairs."

"It's almost perfect, then. The only thing I have to worry about is salesmen fighting over the prime space on the stage."

"You haven't talked to the vendors about their booth space yet?"

"I figured I'd do it when they arrived," Daniel said. "Isn't that how these things always work?"

Donna stared at the junior consul incredulously. "You don't remember all of the planning we did for the last trade show?"

"I remember you and the ambassador talking about moving around tables and which vendors to put next to each other," Daniel said nonchalantly. "I thought all that rearranging furniture and telling people where to sit was just something women do for fun."

"I'm going to pretend I didn't hear that," Kelly said, emerging from her office. "Are you finalizing the floor plan for the show?"

"Daniel just reconfirmed the reservations and we were about to get started on the trade show booth assignments," Donna replied. "He decided to hold the whole conference in the Galaxy room and to use the floor space under the seating for the show and the smaller conference sessions. We'll probably go half and half, since the area under the seats is so large, and the convention center supplies all the temporary walls you want to create different-sized spaces.

"Good idea," Kelly said. "The Empire really whacks you for the first day of any rental, so doing it all in the one room should save a bundle. Am I still on the hook for the keynote?"

"Well, they're expecting you," Daniel said, after a brief hesitation to marvel at how smoothly Donna had covered for his mistake. "If you don't think you can do sixty minutes, we can..."

"Sixty minutes?" Kelly interrupted, her voice rising an octave. "Do you know how many words that is? My weekly reports only average around five minutes, and besides, you're the one who's supposed to be the expert on these people and their communities. What can I possibly talk about for an hour?"

"I was going to suggest that you find some people to act as an economic development panel, and then you could do a little introduction and moderate the discussion. The one thing I'm sure of is that the attendees are more interested in business than politics."

"How am I supposed to find a panel of human economic and business experts on one week's notice?" Kelly demanded disingenuously, watching Donna out of the corner of her eye.

"Was that a rhetorical question, or were you requesting a favor?" Donna inquired sweetly.

"If you get me Stanley and the girls, I'll owe you big."

"Isn't three from one family being a little greedy?"

"They all have different last names now so it won't be obvious," Kelly replied. "Maybe I can get Blythe to wear a disguise so people won't notice that she and Chastity are sisters. She is a spy after all."

"I guess I can get you my father-in-law and either Shaina or Brinda," Daniel offered. "That covers retail and the auction business."

"Then we have a deal, but it will have to be your wife," Kelly said. "Brinda is going along with Lynx and Woojin to the Cayl homeworld to check on business opportunities. I'll try to find one more person to get the panel up to six. Keep up the good work on the conference and let me know if you have any problems."

The ambassador ducked back into her office and smiled as the door slid shut behind her. After racking her brain all morning trying to come up with ideas for a speech, she had given up and decided to talk Daniel into going with a panel presentation instead. It was much better with the idea coming from him.

Immediately after she sat down, "Collect call from mother," appeared floating before her eyes. Collect? "Accept charges," Kelly said out loud, wondering if her mother had lost her wealth by over-leveraging her real-estate investments.

"Is everything all right?" Kelly asked before her mother could even speak.

"If you're wondering why I'm calling collect after we talked just yesterday, it's because Dorothy's job cost me a pair of direct tunnel tickets to come see you. We're on the elevator to orbit now and we should be there by Friday."

"You're coming to see us? That's great. Samuel is always talking about grandma and grandpa, even though he hasn't seen you in years. But what did Dorothy's job have to do with it?"

"You know how your father loves to fish. Dorothy told him a story about some alien fishing rod that came into their lost-and-found. This morning he woke up and insisted we visit Union Station immediately to buy one. I tried to convince him to let Joe do the shopping and send it in the diplomatic pouch, but he wasn't having any of it."

"And that's it? You agreed?"

"Kelly, I've been putting off telling you this, but your father has been going through some changes."

"What do you mean?"

"The doctors have some fancy name for it, but I think it's just old age. His long-term memory is fine, but he has trouble remembering whether he ate breakfast. He also makes impulsive decisions about going places, and if I try to talk him out of it, he gets terribly upset and depressed. A couple of months ago he insisted we visit your sister during their family ski trip in Switzerland, and of course, he spent the whole week sitting in the lodge watching sports because the cold took him by surprise. He's almost ninety you know, and it's a miracle he can still pull on hip waders and walk into a stream with your brother."

"Is he, uh, still all there?" Kelly asked quietly.

"Some days, yes. Other days, well, I just wait for tomorrow."

"Maybe it's a good thing you're coming here, then. Some of the aliens and AI are getting pretty good at human biology, and their technology and pharmacology are way in advance of anything on Earth."

"Have you forgotten that your father and I both have NAT orders?"

"Yeah, but I thought that 'No Alien Technology' just applied to artificial organs and limb replacements, the heavy stuff. If they can do something…"

"Kelly. Your father and I were both born before the Stryx opened Earth, and we decided years ago that we're comfortable drawing the line at human-only medical assistance. Would you want your father choosing to go into stasis for a thousand years in hopes of a cure, or having his mind transferred to a robot made to look human, like those crazy people with too much money and not enough sense?"

"None of us would want that, Mom," Kelly replied, recalling her experiences with dead-end species in Libbyland. "So is there anything special we can plan for while you're here?"

"Well, I'm afraid your father read something into Dorothy's story that wasn't there. When he broods on things, he tends to invent details to make his decisions more attractive."

"Should I talk to the shop owners and make sure they sell him one of those rods cheap?" Kelly guessed. "We can go back and pay the difference afterwards."

"No, it's not the price. He's convinced himself that Union Station is a fisherman's paradise."

"But it's a space station! I know it's so big that you can forget that once you're here, but—hang on. Now that I think of it, we did see some fish on our Libbyland vacation."

"He's strictly catch-and-release at this point, so as long as the fish aren't alien diplomats, anything that lives in the water and swallows artificial flies will be fine," Kelly's mother said hopefully.

"I'll see what I can do, Mom. How about for you? Just because the trip was his idea doesn't mean you should spend the whole time babysitting. Besides, Samuel is nine years old now, and he's pretty good at keeping himself and his Stryx friend busy."

"Well, you know I've been running a club for investors in our retirement city. Everybody is always talking about the opportunities on new worlds, getting in on the ground floor. It's exciting to be part of something like that, even if we won't be around to see the results."

"Is this club for people who have a couple thousand creds to spare, or are there other members like you who've made a killing since the elevators got built?"

"It's a mix, but there are a number of wealthy members with serious amounts of capital who've tried direct investments with the Dollnicks and the Drazens. A couple of them have gotten their fingers badly burned due to cultural misunderstandings, and it's not so easy to keep up with fast-moving developments light-years from Earth."

"You should have told me about this before. Donna's daughters are both in the information business, and the embassy subscribes to their premium services. We'll sit down with Dorothy while you're here and she can help set up some filters to watch for the opportunities you're interested in. She's really good with the holo-interfaces."

"That's very thoughtful of you, Kelly. Tell me something. Do you have any connections with humans who are involved in opening new worlds? As much as I enjoy talking with your alien friends, it would be a real feather in my cap if I could bring my club some off-world investment ideas they could understand. We joined a new umbrella group last year that coordinates large funds for more than a thousand investment clubs worldwide. If you know anybody, it would be worth their time to hear me out."

"Mom? Have you ever considered appearing on a business panel? I think I can get EarthCent Intelligence to pick up the cost of Dad's fishing vacation."

Six

"How come I've never been in here before?" Kelly asked the ceiling. The elegant meeting room was located at one end of the immense cylindrical space station, with a transparent wall or atmosphere retention field that allowed the occupants to look out over the traffic entering and leaving the hollow core. The chairs around the table, which at first looked like a mismatched collection, turned out to be custom built for the ambassadors of the different species, complete with name tags.

"The other ambassadors don't have a contractual obligation to participate in our open house," Libby replied. "If you held the meeting at your embassy, I doubt you would have had much luck convincing some of them to host a visiting emissary. We use this room when we call for a special meeting, which hasn't happened since you've been ambassador. It will remind the others that we're the ones who are asking for a favor."

"But I've been on the station almost twenty years. It seems like a terrible waste to let a room like this sit unused."

"It wouldn't have the same impact if we rented it out for weddings or private parties and everybody had been here before. Srythlan and the Grenouthian ambassador have both been on the station long enough to have attended the last special meeting we called, but it will be the first time for the others."

"What was that meeting about?" Kelly asked. She circled the large oval table, checking how the placement of platters from the caterer lined up with the labeled chairs of the species, and she had to admit that Donna couldn't have planned it better.

"A dispute over a star system with one world settled by the Hortens and another by the Drazens. We generally resolve conflicts between tunnel network members by decree, but I convinced Gryph that the ambassadors present on Union Station at that time would make the right decision if he asked them to judge the case on its merits."

"You were wrong?"

"Let's just say I wasn't right. The Hortens spent more on bribes than the Drazens and were awarded the system. To prevent hard feelings, Gryph provided the Drazens with a similar unoccupied system from his hidden reserve."

"All's well that ends well," Kelly said, peeling back the plastic wrap from a tray and extracting one of her favorite faux-chicken salad roll-ups.

"I'm the one who had to pay Gryph back for the system he gave up," Libby told her. "He said it would teach me an important lesson."

"A lesson for the teacher," Kelly marveled. "I never realized that the Stryx held private assets the same way as everybody else."

"Why do you think I charge Blythe and Chastity to handle the bookings for InstaSitter?" Libby asked. "My dating service is very expensive to run, so it's never really made much of a profit. Now I'm hoping that with the theme park, I'll be able to pay Gryph back ahead of schedule."

"Did Jeeves put you up to that explanation? I can't even tell when you're being serious anymore."

Gwendolyn chose that moment to enter the room, and the Stryx librarian left Kelly's question unanswered.

"Gwen, you're ten minutes early," Kelly greeted the Gem ambassador.

"I thought you might need help with the arrangements but it looks like everything is set."

"You're seated next to me, and the mixed assortment of chocolates is between us."

Gwendolyn smiled, and then hesitated for a moment before asking, "Is it a bad time to talk about something unrelated to the open house?"

"Not at all. What is it, Gwen?"

"I'm worried about Mist," Gwendolyn said with a sigh. "When Dorothy came over the other day, they talked about boys nonstop."

"That's normal for sixteen-year olds," Kelly replied. Then it hit her that there weren't any Gem males for Mist to be interested in. "Oh, I'm sorry, Gwen," she said, taking the clone's hand. "I didn't think before I spoke. But even though Mist imitates Dorothy in some of her clothing choices, she never seems to be confused about her species identity. And what could we do about it anyway?"

"I'm thinking about resigning as ambassador and taking Mist back to one of our worlds. The project to restore the other bloodlines from our race using the genetic samples obtained from the Farlings is moving along rapidly. Originally, the goal was to clone as many individuals as possible to reestablish our genetic diversity, but there's a growing movement to just clone the males for the time being, until there are enough to go around for the

63

living Gem who want to experience marriage and natural conception."

"But what about the age difference?" Kelly asked, after getting over her immediate reaction of disbelief. The Gem were the galaxy's champion cloners, and if anybody could build a population of men to order, it was them.

"We live longer than humans," Gwendolyn replied self-consciously. "Almost all of the other sentients do, it's just something that develops in species over time. But you know that since we ejected the old elites and their status quo, we've begun incorporating alien technology and sciences into our culture. Now everybody's talking about the new stasis hotels that are springing up, and I think I should suggest it to Mist."

"A stasis hotel? You mean, you check-in, they put you to sleep, and you remain in stasis until you get a wake-up call?"

"And the hotels are working with the crèche worlds so that they can plan on reviving customers when there are sufficient males of a suitable age. Some of my sisters argue that we should raise the boys so they look favorably on entering plural marriages with older women, or that we should ask them to donate their, you know, for Gem who want to become pregnant."

"Are these stasis hotels available to everybody, or is there a selection process?"

"Like a clone beauty contest? That would be a bit dull," Gwendolyn said with a laugh. "Besides, Mist is a hero in the Gem Empire for winning hide-and-seek at the Carnival and financing our purchases from Farling Pharmaceutical with her prize. One of the reasons I accepted the ambassadorship here rather than returning home was so Mist could enjoy being a teenager without all of the adulation. If she wants to go into stasis, they'll put her at the top of the wake-up list."

"I don't know what to tell you," Kelly said. "We'll miss her, we'll miss both of you if you go, but to give her a chance at a normal life? Have you been doing anything to prepare her for a talk about this?"

"Not yet. I thought I'd wait until Dorothy starts dating so Mist can have a clear picture of the choice she's making," Gwendolyn replied. "Oh, the other ambassadors are starting to arrive."

Bork and Czeros entered the room side by side, both of them ogling at the view.

"Srythlan told me about this room," Bork said. "It's a shame they don't rent it out for special events."

"Do either of you know what this meeting is about?" Czeros asked the women. "Bork says he knows but he won't say, and I think he's making it up."

"The Stryx didn't tell you?" Kelly asked.

"Just a request to attend a special meeting about the open house, and that there would be a pricey California Cabernet available," the Frunge ambassador replied. "And there it is." He headed for the table and set to work uncorking the first bottle.

"Ambassadors," announced a gorgeous Vergallian woman as she strode up to the table. "I am Aluria, and I assume you will all accept this introduction as a substitute for an official reception at our embassy."

"I heard that our last Vergallian ambassador had moved on," Bork said. "Did she leave the embassy so messy that you're embarrassed to invite us all over?"

"The embassy underwent renovations during the transition period and the ballroom is now somewhat smaller, so

I'm forced to be selective about my guest lists," Aluria replied coldly.

Bork's tentacle began to rise in anger and Czeros looked up from the cheese platter with a frown, but Kelly walked over to Aluria and offered her hand. After a moment's hesitation, the Vergallian ambassador deigned to brush fingers in the manner of a superior acknowledging a subordinate. The Grenouthian ambassador had since entered the room and he hopped right over to the Vergallian.

"Aluria. So nice to see you again."

"Ambassador," Aluria replied warmly. "I hope you'll be available for my official reception."

"Of course," the giant bunny replied. "My wife and her grooming circle friends are all looking forward to it."

"Aluria. Thank you for the invitation," Ambassador Crute declared, approaching the group. "My children and their nanny have never been to an official reception before, and they're all very excited."

"My pleasure," the Vergallian ambassador said, turning on the charm. "Ambassador Srythlan. We haven't been properly introduced, but I hope you and your family will be able to attend my official reception."

"A prior engagement," the Verlock ambassador replied slowly, not altering the straight line he had taken towards his seat at the table. "Perhaps one of my junior staff might attend."

Aluria's beautiful face flashed red and then white, so quickly that a casual observer could be forgiven for confusing her with a Horten. Then Ortha arrived, his skin tinged blue, and the Vergallian's creamy complexion returned to its normal, flawless state.

"Aluria, my dear," the Horten ambassador said. "Your arrival on Union Station was much anticipated, and I look forward to renewing the close relations that existed between myself and your predecessor."

"Of course," Aluria replied, having completely recovered the poise she had lost at Srythlan's obvious slight. "Quite the little gathering the Stryx have invited us to. I wonder what's on the agenda?"

The Chert ambassador appeared in his chair, the ever-present invisibility projector perched on his shoulder, and Kelly did a quick head count to compare with the number of seats.

"Ambassador Ptew has a family emergency and won't be able to attend," Libby announced. "Everybody please be seated and give your attention to Ambassador McAllister, the host of our upcoming open house."

"Those polygamous birds always have a family emergency," Ortha said in an undertone as he took his seat.

"Thank you, Libby," Kelly said, ignoring Ortha's rudeness. "As the contractual host of the upcoming open house, the Stryx have asked me to arrange lodgings with ambassadors on this station for the visiting emissaries. This group will be arriving in advance of the body of guests, and while we won't try to keep it a secret, I hope I can count on you not to publicize their presence until the open house officially begins."

"I will waive my claim to the honor of entertaining a foreign dignitary in the interest of group harmony," Ortha declared immediately, not bothering to keep the sarcasm from his voice. Several of the other ambassadors silently cursed themselves for having immediately dug into the food and being constrained from speaking until they could swallow.

"You do realize that it's the Stryx making this request, not me," Kelly said, taking advantage of catering-induced silence. "Our station librarian tells me that if we do a good job entertaining the emissaries from the Cayl Empire, it will greatly increase the odds of their joining the tunnel network, en masse. I have already offered to put up all five of the visiting dignitaries myself, but the Stryx…"

"The Stryx have more sense than to gamble on humans to make a good impression," Aluria interrupted. "The Empire of a Hundred Worlds has had contact with the Cayl Empire in the past and we will not be cheated out of our rights. I will host the Lood emissary, though I'll thank him to keep his mask on."

"Perhaps I spoke too hastily," Ortha said, turning a pinkish white. "After all, it's not every day one has the opportunity to spend quality time with a diplomatic colleague from the other side of the galaxy. I seem to recall a species with silver skin from a Grenouthian documentary, and I'm sure we could make their emissary feel at home and, uh, influence the, uh, outcome."

"Is one of the visiting emissaries a Nangor?" Crute asked, spitting some crumbs into the air as he rushed into the fray. "We have occasionally traded with them in the past, despite the distance, as not many species manufacture tools and equipment that suit a four-armed operator. I'm sure it would be an error on your part to place a Nangor with anybody else."

"I didn't receive any special instructions from the Stryx, so I guess 'First come, first serve,' is appropriate," Kelly said. "I will be hosting the Cayl at Libby's request, so that just leaves the turtles, I mean, the Tzvim."

"I," Srythlan began, but the Grenouthian ambassador spoke right over him.

"Of course we will host the Tzvim. It's safe to say that over the last hundred thousand years, my people have had more contact with the members of the Cayl Empire than any of the other species present. It's only appropriate we should have the opportunity to return the hospitality they have shown our documentary crews."

The translation of his last sentence came through Kelly's implant sounding oddly like a threat, but she brushed the thought aside.

"I would have offered to invite the Tzvim emissary, but we are allergic to their epidermal shedding," Srythlan finally got out.

"Well, this was much easier than I anticipated," Kelly remarked happily. She had come into the meeting worried that she would have to lean on her friends to accept a mismatched guest, but instead, the ambassadors from the species who usually gave her a hard time had stepped up.

"If that's everything, I have a party to finish planning," Aluria announced, rising from her seat. "We in the Empire of a Hundred Worlds are always happy to do our part for the Stryx."

"Likewise," Crute declared, pushing back from the table. "Can I assume that nobody else intended to partake in this gourmet platter of Sheezle bugs? Good. I'll just take it with me then."

"Yes. I just remembered I have something as well," Ortha stated. He didn't rise from the table immediately because he was busy wrapping Horten delicacies in napkins and slipping them into his pockets. "For the children," he added, addressing no one in particular.

"Since everybody else is leaving," the Grenouthian ambassador said. His pouch looked strangely lumpy as he hopped away, and Kelly noted that the platters in front of his seat were swept clean, even though the ambassadors had only been seated for a couple of minutes.

"Where's the fire?" Czeros called after them. He uncorked a second bottle of California Cabernet, and shocked Kelly by pouring glasses for Bork, Gwendolyn and herself before filling his own. A sound like stones being crushed into gravel came from the end of the table, and everybody turned to see the Verlock caught in a rare fit of laughter, his massive shoulders heaving.

"Am I missing something here?" Kelly demanded. "I know that Vergallians and the Dollnicks do a lot of business outside of the tunnel network, that the Hortens are a bit slippery and the Grenouthians think they're smarter than everybody else, but why did they all agree to help me?"

"Your little speech was a marvel of underhanded motivation, though it took a moment for them to figure it out," the Chert ambassador explained. "They aren't used to subtlety from humans."

"But I was being perfectly honest," Kelly said. "By taking home an alien dignitary, they're doing a favor for the Stryx."

"Why would they do favors for the Stryx?" Bork asked. "Will the Stryx give them special treatment in return? It was your remark about the station librarian that woke up Aluria, and the rest of them figured it out as soon as she spoke."

"Figured what out?" Kelly asked in frustration.

"That their best chance of affecting the decisions of the visiting emissaries is to get them alone, on their own turf," Czeros said. "The Cayl Empire is a completely functional entity that's been around for millions of years. Do you know what that means?"

"They're stable?" Kelly said.

"They're competition," Srythlan boomed.

"Imagine what will happen if the Stryx push a permanent tunnel through to the other side of the galaxy," the Chert ambassador continued. "All of a sudden, the members of the Cayl Empire with expansionist tendencies will be able to send their colony ships to the systems on the fringes of the tunnel network for little more cost than expanding the edges of their own empire."

"The Dollnicks and the Vergallians are the most expansionist of the oxygen/nitrogen breathing species on the tunnel network," Bork explained. "The Grenouthians practically have a monopoly on news, documentary entertainment and several other business verticals with high entry costs, and the Hortens operate in the gray areas of tunnel network membership through the agency of their off-network pirate cousins. All of them have counterparts doing the same thing in the Cayl Empire. The last thing they want is competition."

"But it's not a zero-sum game," Kelly protested. "Whatever opportunities the Cayl Empire members find on our side of the galaxy, our species can pursue on their side."

"That assumes a level playing field, which is highly unlikely," Czeros said. "No matter what the agreed-upon terms, the Cayl Empire will not transform into the tunnel network overnight. For the duration of the transitional period, which will likely stretch for thousands of years, the advantage will go to the members of the former Cayl Empire."

"And I just handed over the visiting emissaries to the four species on the station who want them to reject joining up?"

"Try a glass of this Cabernet," Gwendolyn suggested. "It's pretty strong."

"Don't feel bad," the Verlock rumbled. "The visiting diplomats aren't from the nicest species. I doubt any of them would have survived this long without the Cayl making all of their important decisions for them."

Seven

"You're so lucky," said Hert, the Drazen boy who Dorothy relieved at the lost-and-found. "The new shelving unit is nearly in place. I bet it furls its dustcover on your shift."

"Really?" Dorothy said. She ran down the space behind the counter to see if Hert's prediction was accurate. Sure enough, the shelving unit which had been inching its way up from the back and had been well into the final turn during her last shift was now almost parallel with the other shelving units in the front row. As soon as it moved into place, the dust cover would retract and the unit would become available for stocking. She tried a tentative push to encourage progress, but there was no give in the mechanism.

"Not much came in today," Hert continued, after following her down the counter at a more leisurely pace. "The top shelf of the current unit is practically empty, but the rule is to start at the bottom of the next one as soon as it becomes available."

"Why's that?" Dorothy asked.

"Just the way the system is set up, I guess. The Verlock kid who used to have the shift before me claimed that the Stryx will speed up the whole train to keep the value of the items on any one shelving unit from getting too high. I guess they aren't that happy with the prices they get when they put the back row out to bid."

"But I thought that auctions were supposed to be the ideal mechanism for price discovery," Dorothy said. The Drazen boy stared at her in bewilderment, as if his implant had failed to translate her words into anything sensible. "My family has friends in the auction business and that's what they always say. It means that the only price that matters in the market is what people are willing to pay."

"Thanks, that makes sense now. Well, I'd stick around to see the new unit open up since we're lucky to get two a year, but I have a presentation tomorrow so I've got to get going."

"Alright. Bye, Hert."

After the Drazen boy left, Dorothy put her lunch in the small refrigeration cabinet provided for the staff. She checked the plastic bins at the end of the counter to see if Hert had left her any items to catalog and shelve, but they were empty. Dorothy had already reached the point where she preferred catching a shift after some of the lazier kids so that she'd have something to do when she came in, but she supposed that getting used to boring jobs was part of being a grownup.

A loud 'click' sounded behind her, and she spun around to see that the new shelving unit had fully arrived. The dust cover began to retract, a small motor furling the previously taut fabric towards a cavity at the very top of the case. Dorothy sat on the counter and watching in excitement as the receding cover revealed clean, bare shelves. In a few minutes, it was all over.

"Well, that was something," she remarked, half laughing at herself for having sat enthralled by the show. Not having anything else to do, she stepped onto the small lift platform for the shelving unit and took it up to the top to examine the furled roll. Something strange about the angle of the top shelf where it met the back of the unit caught her eye, and she reached all the way into the corner to identify the anomaly. Her hand found a rounded metallic shape, cool to the touch. She felt that the center of the object was hollow, and hoping that it wasn't a manual pull-cord to activate a fire suppression system or trigger the emergency ejection of the shelving unit from the station, she gave it a tug.

Out in the light, the piece turned out to be a strangely carved bracelet, though the details were difficult to make out since the whole thing was black. She turned it over in her hand and felt a sort of a tingle in her fingers, as if the object was generating some sort of energy field. Dorothy repeated the English translation of the Verlock nomenclature for the location on the shelf several times so she wouldn't forget it. Then she ordered the lift platform back down and placed the object on the turntable for scanning.

"Bracelet discovered on shelving unit LEV, location 20/27," she said, giving the turntable a spin.

"Item not in inventory," the cataloging system's voice replied.

"What do you mean it's not in inventory? I just took it off the shelf."

"Shelving unit LEV is empty," the voice insisted.

"Libby? Can you explain to our cataloging system that I found something on the top shelf of the new unit that must have been missed by whoever cleaned it out."

"The cataloging system isn't sentient," Libby replied. "I'll take over for a moment and perform a scan." A beam of light traced the contours of the object, and then several more beams of different colors which Dorothy hadn't seen utilized before joined in the analysis. A minute went by, and then two.

"Libby? Don't you know what it is?" Dorothy asked.

"It's a bracelet," the Stryx librarian replied dryly, but the light beams continued to flicker and probe. "There. It's safe now if you want to keep it."

"I can have it? But what if the owner comes looking for it?"

"The bracelet was left behind on the shelf, either accidentally or intentionally, by the Frunge who purchased the lot at auction more than twenty-three years ago. There are exactly two hundred and fifty rows of shelves in the room, so how long is an item on the shelves before it goes to auction?"

"Does it always take twenty-three years for a full row to move back one rank?"

"You can assume twenty-three as an average."

"So two hundred and fifty rows means almost fifty-eight hundred years. That's a long time."

"While there are many advanced species with life-spans in excess of that number, we feel no obligation to hold onto every lost item against the chance somebody might come around six thousand years from now looking for it."

"But how about the Frunge who bought the auction lot?" Dorothy asked.

"The purchase agreement specifies that all buyers must clean out any shelving unit for which they are the high bidder. We could penalize the Frunge who purchased the lot for not fulfilling his obligation, but he's no longer on Union Station, and it's hardly worth pursuing in any case."

"Did you say something about the bracelet maybe being left behind on purpose?"

"The Frunge may have recognized it as a protective amulet of the Teragram cult and decided it was safer not to touch it. Although they rarely visit the tunnel network, the Teragram mages play an outsized role in the mythology of some of the advanced species, including the Frunge."

"You mean it's magic?" Dorothy retrieved the bracelet from the turntable and held it up for closer examination. The black metal it was formed from seemed to drink in the light and not let any escape. She could feel the runes carved into the surface, but they seemed to swim together before her eyes when she tried to pick out the specific shapes.

"The Teragram mages relied primarily on technological tricks to impress less advanced species. I've disabled the bracelet's offensive capabilities so you can't accidentally cause any harm."

Dorothy slipped the alien artifact over her hand and was somewhat surprised to find that it felt lighter on her wrist. She swung her arm around a few times, admiring the contrast between the unknown metal and her own fair skin. Then she heard a polite cough from the intake end of the counter.

"Coming," Dorothy sang, and practically skipped across the room.

A skinny human boy, perhaps a year older than herself, waited patiently for her. He was dressed in a worn set of coveralls which had the bleached look of laundered work-clothes from the take-it-or-leave-it booth that EarthCent sponsored on the Shuk deck for needy humans. A deep tan suggested that he had spent a good deal of his life outside before arriving on Union Station.

"Cool bracelet," the boy said, his sharp eyes having followed Dorothy's own repeated looks at her wrist.

77

"Thank you. Have you lost something?"

"Yeah," the boy said, his eyes shifting from the girl, to the shelves behind her, and back to the girl again in rapid succession. "Can I look through the shelves for it?"

"That stuff has been here for years," Dorothy said with a smile. "You have to tell me what it is you've lost and I'll find it for you if it's here. If you remember when you lost it, I'll know where to start looking."

"Wouldn't it be easier if I just looked myself?" the boy said smoothly, though Dorothy thought she saw a disappointed look flee across his face.

"We can't let anybody behind the counter. It would help if you tell me your name and describe the object."

"My whole name?" the boy asked suspiciously.

"Your first name is fine. It's just so I can call you something. I'm Dorothy."

"David." He hesitated for a moment, and then he extended an arm over the counter. The two teenagers exchanged an awkward handshake. "I lost my, uh, I had ten creds this morning and, uh…" he trailed off.

"Let me look," Dorothy said, feeling her face turning hot as she grew embarrassed for him. She had heard from the other employees about space bums coming into the lost-and-found to look for supposedly lost wallets and purses. Normally they had the sense to window-shop at a few boutiques first so they could at least describe a popular change-purse, though they usually tripped up when questioned about the contents.

"This bin has the smaller stuff that's come in so far today," she continued, lifting it onto the counter. "We don't get a lot of money coming through here though. I guess that's because there are plenty of dishonest people who would just pick it up and keep it." She glanced up at the end of the sentence without really meaning to, and caught the boy looking like he wanted to crawl into a hole and die.

Dorothy turned her attention back to the bin, hiding her own face as she pawed through the contents. "There's some sort of tool kit, you wouldn't want that. Alien something, alien something, alien something. Dental floss? Alien something, alien something, oh, here's a change purse."

"It's not mine," the boy mumbled.

Dorothy looked up and saw that he had edged halfway to the door, as if he was preparing to make a run for it.

"It's not very heavy," she said, weighing it in one hand. Without looking down, she thumbed open the magnet seal and poured the contents out in her hand. "Look, it's six coins. A five-cred and five one-creds."

"It's not mine," David repeated in a choked voice, looking truly miserable. "I'm sorry, I have to go."

"Wait," Dorothy said, setting the coins down next to the change purse and coming around the counter to catch him at the door. Up close, she was surprised to find that he was a half a head taller than her. She kept forgetting that the floor behind the counter was raised. "I want—I need a favor. Can you do a favor for me?"

"What?" The boy sounded like he had just witnessed somebody being beaten and had not intervened.

"I'm here for another five hours and I forgot to bring my lunch today," Dorothy lied. "I thought maybe I'd send out for a pizza, but I only have five creds, and with the delivery charge and tip, it leaves me short."

"I don't have any money," David said in the same monotone.

79

"I'm not asking for money," Dorothy said, instinctively omitting her trademarked "Silly," at the last second. "If you go and get it, I'll have enough and we can split it. I can't eat a whole pizza by myself."

"I'm not a charity case," the boy mumbled, his ears flaming.

"It's not charity, you'll be doing me a favor," Dorothy insisted, her voice rising forcefully. She reached in her own change purse, rapidly sorted through the coins by feel, and prayed that the one she pulled out was a five-cred, and not the twenty-cred her mother insisted she carry for emergencies. Dorothy glanced at it to make sure she had guessed right and pressed it into his hand. "Fabio's Fabulous Pizzeria. It's in the Little Apple, like ten steps from the lift-tube bank."

David lifted his head a little, but he wouldn't look directly at her. "What do you want on it?"

"The five-cred special, it's loaded with stuff. Some days it comes with free drinks, but I forget which. It doesn't matter since we have water here."

David looked at her full in the face now, and his mouth worked but he didn't say anything. His eyes were wet.

"Go!" she said, pushing him into the corridor. After making sure he left, she went back behind the counter, returned the six coins to the change purse, and replaced it in the bin. Then she looked through the rest of the items just to familiarize herself with what had come in, and put the bin back in its place below the counter.

Forty-five minutes went by before somebody finally came in, the leader of a Drazen choral group looking for her ornate pitch pipe. The woman had left it unattended for just a minute in a public access practice room, where it was collected by an overeager maintenance bot. The

80

Drazen was so happy to find the instrument that she insisted on voicing her thanks to the girl, who struggled to look enthusiastic as the singer attempted a piece that was intended for a full choir.

Once she was alone again, Dorothy fought against the urge to ask Libby for news about David. She knew that the Stryx librarian could easily locate him through the surveillance system, but she had never requested that sort of favor before and didn't know if it was really appropriate. She didn't care about the five creds, but she would have liked to see the boy eat something. Thinking about food made her feel hungry herself, but she had already decided not to touch her lunch in the refrigerator since it would be too awful if he did return and caught her in a lie.

A young Dollnick came in looking for the missing mitt from a paddle-cup-mitt-ball set, which he had last used on the all-species park deck that had formerly belonged to the Gem. He couldn't remember exactly which day it had been, but Dorothy recalled seeing a Dollnick mitt fairly recently and found it in a bin halfway down the counter. The Dollnick boy tried it on to make sure it was his, thanked her, and left without tipping.

An hour after she had given up on ever seeing David again, he appeared suddenly, a bag with two drinks dangling awkwardly from the finger of one of the hands supporting the pizza box.

"Sorry it took so long," he apologized, before she could speak. "They weren't open yet when I got there, I guess they don't get enough business in the morning on human time. I looked around for somewhere else, but the only places I found were full service restaurants that didn't have a pizza for five creds. I was passing Fabio's on my way back just as the owner got there, but it took a long while for the oven to heat up. It wasn't a free drink day, but he gave me these for waiting."

"I knew it was something like that," Dorothy said, bending the truth for the second time in less than two hours. Her mother always said that the only time it was alright to lie to people was to spare their feelings, so she figured neither of her transgressions counted. Her father said that lying was also permissible to save a life, play poker, or to keep her mother from getting upset.

"I didn't know what you would want to drink, so I got an orange soda and a cola," David continued, removing the covered cups, napkins, and even a packet of pepper from the bag.

"I like them both," Dorothy said, even though she preferred water to soda. "Open up the box and let it start cooling. Pizza stays hot forever in those things."

David pulled back the cover and the smell of fresh baked pizza flooded the room. The appetite Dorothy thought she had lost came roaring back, but she had experienced enough blisters on the roof of her mouth to force herself to wait. She had a hundred questions she wanted to ask the boy, but she was afraid he was so sensitive that he might run off before he ate. She bit the inside of her cheek and waited for him to speak first.

"Have you lived on Union Station a long time?" he finally asked.

"I was born here. My mother is the EarthCent ambassador and my father runs all sorts of businesses in the hold we rent. My older brother is an engineer, and he's currently designing rides for the Libbyland theme park with Jeeves, his Stryx friend. I came up with the Libbyland name when we vacationed there before it opened. I have a little brother too, but he's only nine so he still goes to school. Did you go to school?"

David shook his head, still processing the information dump.

"Did you have a teacher bot? Paul's wife, Aisha, grew up on Earth, and she came from a poor village where they had teacher bots, since the Stryx provide them almost for free. She's really smart, and she has a popular show for kids on the Grenouthian network, 'Let's Make Friends,' though she never uses any of my ideas. She says they aren't age-appropriate." Dorothy concluded with a head toss, indicating what she thought of her sister-in-law's judgment.

"Oh," David replied.

He looked a little strange, and suddenly it occurred to Dorothy that he might think she was making it all up. Now that she put herself in his shoes, it did seem a bit hard to believe that a girl working in a lost-and-found would be the daughter of the ambassador and sister-in-law of the most famous human in the galaxy. She wondered for a second if people from Union Station who had never met Aisha claimed to know her.

"It's funny how people clump together," Dorothy said, introducing her favorite theory without realizing she was digging a deeper credibility hole. "Lynx, one of our spy friends, says that if everybody kept track of all the coincidences in our lives, we'd end up believing that we're guided by an unseen hand. But Uncle Stanley says that the whole invisible hand business is part of a disproven economic theory from centuries ago. Of course, my mom thinks she sees the hand and it belongs to the Stryx."

"I don't think I understand," David replied honestly, but she saw that he was staring at her like she had hypnotized him.

"Oh, let's eat the pizza before it gets cold!"

"You first," the boy insisted, so she pulled out a slice, taking part of the toppings from the slice next to it in her haste. David took a slice from the other side, folded it, and began chewing energetically. He finished before she was halfway through her slice, and trembled like a horse in the starting gate while he waited for her to catch up before taking his next serving.

When she realized what he was doing, Dorothy said, "You don't have to wait for me. I can only eat three slices at the most, anyway."

"Are you sure?" he asked, even as he lifted and folded the next piece.

Dorothy nodded, and the pizza rapidly disappeared. They finished at the same time, even though he ate five slices to her three.

"Thank you," Dorothy said, keeping up the fiction that he had done her a favor. She tried to recall all of the lessons about getting information out of people she had gleaned from watching Chance train spies for EarthCent Intelligence. Start by asking something innocuous so he doesn't get defensive, she remembered. "So, are you planning on staying on Union Station for a while?"

"If I can find a job," David replied. He turned serious, a full belly having done wonders for his confidence. "You can tell that I'm a contract runner, can't you?"

"I guessed. You're safe on the station, though. The Stryx don't allow bounty hunters to work here. It's only until you're eighteen, right?"

"I'll probably be clear in another year. It seems like for-ever."

"Well, getting a job is easy," Dorothy declared confidently, "I know lots of people. Would you rather work in a restaurant, an open market or a theme park? You're too young to be a spy."

Eight

"It looks a bit like the Coliseum in Rome, but in better condition." Kelly's mother surveyed the Galaxy room of the Empire Convention Center with a critical eye and tried to estimate the capacity. "What does it seat? Ten thousand?"

"Maybe half that with a mixed alien crowd, I'm not sure about the count when it's all humans," Daniel replied. "I have no idea how many people will show up this morning, but I think we'll get the majority of the official delegates."

"How many official delegates are there?"

"Just over two hundred, Marge," the junior consul replied. "Most of them are mayors from open worlds with a number of sovereign human communities. But the first priority with all of these people is growing their economies, so they send trade delegations as well. EarthCent Intelligence picked up the tab for up to five additional attendees for each official delegate, meaning we could get over a thousand people this morning."

"And the other panel members are all Kelly's friends?"

"Yep. My wife Shaina is going to be on the panel. She arrived with me but she's checking on the setup for the trade fair in the galleries under the seats."

"I think they're called arcades," Marge replied. "Kelly? Is that right?"

"You're asking me about a vocabulary word, Mom? Uh, I think they're only considered arcades if it's real stone architecture, because the builders used arches to support the seats."

"No arcades without arches," Marge replied agreeably. "Makes sense to me."

Shaina emerged from one of the passages, carrying the baby in a sling across her chest, and came over to where her husband was talking with Kelly's mother. "Hi, Marge. I haven't seen you in ages. Is your husband along this trip?"

"Yes, he is, but he doesn't have the patience for this sort of thing anymore. He's back in Mac's Bones with Joe and my grandson, and they're all practicing casting with his new fishing rod."

"Sounds like fun," Shaina said. "How long do we have?"

"Another fifteen minutes," Daniel replied.

"Don't disappear at the last minute," she warned him. "You have to take the baby when I'm on."

"Ahem," Jeeves announced himself, floating up to the small group. "Are you sure you don't want me on your panel? I'm very good at questions and answers."

"You're very good at avoiding questions and making up answers," Kelly retorted. "This is going to be an all-human discussion panel, probably the first one I've been involved with since I came here."

Shaina's father arrived and read the place card for his seat on the panel. "Peter Hadad – Kitchen Kitsch President. I've been promoted from a hawker to a president. Great way to start the morning."

"Donna made up the titles," Kelly replied. "Did you see my mom's?"

"Marge Frank – Investment Club Chairman."

"You don't think it sounds a bit too grandiose?" Marge asked.

"Why not chairwoman?" Peter inquired.

"Donna said the two extra letters would force her to shrink the font," Kelly explained.

"Shaina Cohan – SBJ Auctioneers," Peter read his daughter's place card. "I still haven't gotten used to the name change."

"How do you think I feel?" Stanley asked, coming up and putting an arm around Peter's shoulders. He read the place cards for both of his daughters out loud. "Blythe Oxford – EarthCent Intelligence. Chastity Papamarkakis – Free Press. I guess Donna couldn't fit the whole name of the paper after my son-in-law's family name took up all the space."

Delegates began trickling into the Galaxy room to secure seats near the stage facing the panel. Two-thirds of the amphitheatre's seating was taped off to discourage attendees from sitting in areas with bad viewing angles. There was nothing left to do but wait for the starting time, and Kelly took Daniel aside while the panel's elder members began competing over who could tell the most embarrassing story about one of their grown children.

"Did you read my introduction?" she asked her junior consul. "I've been so busy with preparing for the open house that I just dashed something off and sent it to you."

"I'm glad to hear you didn't put in a lot of effort because I think you should drop all of the parts about governing. I know that we're supposed to be helping the sovereign communities build a political alliance, but they barely have governments of their own in place, and they're primarily interested in business ties. I don't think any of them feel like they can take their eyes off the ball and start devoting resources to politics."

"Thank you for being honest," the ambassador said. She pulled out her tab and skimmed through the brief introduction she had written. "Welcome to the Third Annual Conference of Sovereign Human Communities. Uh, scratch this next paragraph, skip that, no, delete, no. Ah. There will be a free luncheon sponsored by EarthCent Intelligence in the food court between noon and 1:00 PM, local human time. Uh, skip, redact, drop, no. Ah. There will be a cocktail reception at 6:00 PM this evening sponsored by the Galactic Free Press. And now, let me introduce our panel members who will be taking questions from the audience."

"Powerful," Daniel said. "You might want to not say anything out loud about the bits you're skipping over."

"Thank you, Daniel. I'll try to keep that in mind."

Twenty minutes later, with her brief opening speech and the panel member introductions out of the way, Kelly fished in the wicker basket filled with questions collected from the official delegates, and pulled one out at random.

"Got any money?" she read.

"Why don't you take this one," Blythe said, nudging Kelly's mother after the laughter died down.

Marge began to speak into the floating microphone, which automatically maintained the optimum distance from her mouth. "Yes, we have money. Investment clubs on Earth have a surprising amount of capital available, thanks in large part to the low cost of living on a half-empty planet. What we lack is a well-regulated market for making off-world investments. A number of prominent club members worldwide have been burned in deals with various species, and it's led to a general reluctance about investing in alien enterprises. But if any of you are interested in visiting Earth and speaking to investors, I'm sure we can put you in front of an attentive audience. Convincing them that you're trustworthy will be up to you."

"I'd like to add something to that," Stanley said. "Most of you are from open worlds controlled by Dollnick merchant princes, Drazen consortiums, or the Verlocks. The merchant princes control their own capital, the Drazen consortiums work through personal relations to gather stakeholders, and the typical Verlock clan will provide backing to any enterprise that presents a mathematical proof of profitability. Humans have traditionally funded new businesses using all three of these methods, but in addition, Earth-based businesses are generally required to provide proof of accountability. I doubt any of you employ Certified Public Accountants to do your books, but they played a big part in convincing human investors in the past that the numbers had something behind them."

"A lot of good that did before the Stryx came," somebody cried out. The thousand-strong audience indulged in a round of laughter.

"Too true," Stanley acknowledged. "But human psychology is a funny thing, and the best mistakes are the ones we repeat over and over again. It would be nice if every potential investor could visit your factories and communities, live with your families and learn to trust you. But a retiree on Earth looking for diversified investments can't justify spending that sort of time or money on off-world travel. I would definitely encourage you to visit Earth and talk to investors, but I would also suggest you start thinking about establishing an agency that could certify your books for humans who will never visit your worlds. I don't have to tell you that such certifications live or die by their track record."

"Hear, hear," somebody called out. A number of whispered conversations started in the audience, accompanied by a lot of nodding heads.

Kelly looked at her panel to see if anybody else wanted to comment, and then fished out the next question.

"Do you have any money?"

The audience burst out laughing again, and the delegates nudged each other in the ribs. Apparently they all had the same thing in mind. Kelly silently read and disposed of a half-dozen randomly selected slips before she found a new question. "What does EarthCent Intelligence get out of all of this?"

"That's me," Blythe said. "We took a bath on the first conference, came near breaking even on the second one, and we expect to be in the black this year. Basically, we're pedaling your contact information to a select and limited group of alien vendors, which will explain for some of you why you've been getting unsolicited sales calls. In addition, the business and demographics information you provide for our database saves a lot of payroll expenses we would otherwise be forced to spend on field agents to gather the same facts. Without this information, our ambassadors would be at a severe disadvantage when negotiating with the very species which control your worlds."

"I'd like to add something to that," Chastity said after her sister finished speaking. "The Galactic Free Press and EarthCent Intelligence are essentially in the same business. Our paper delivers information to subscribers, while EarthCent Intelligence packages and sells data to the business community and retains sensitive political infor-

91

mation exclusively for EarthCent. The Galactic Free Press subscribes to EarthCent Intelligence's basic database so that our reporters and editors can quickly locate the facts to back up their stories."

"Give us an example," Shaina suggested.

"Today we'll be publishing a piece about the two-man floaters manufactured on Chianga, which are being unveiled at this conference. Without the EarthCent Intelligence data on Chiangan manufacturing, pictures from agent visits to that factory, and an intelligence synopsis of the Dollnick technology the floaters are derived from, the story would be little more than a public relations announcement."

Kelly waited a moment to make sure nobody else on the panel had anything to add, and then she withdrew another slip of paper. After glancing at the question, she sighed in an exaggerated fashion. While the audience chuckled, she went through three more entries before finding a question that wasn't about the availability of money or the conference sponsors.

"Here's an interesting one. Do all of the Stryx stations have large human populations, and are there any special requirements to market goods on the stations?"

"Me first," Shaina said quickly, getting the jump on her father. "I've visited over twenty Stryx stations in the last few years to conduct auctions, and I'd say that most of them had larger human populations than we have here. It's mainly a question of proximity to systems where large numbers of humans are working for aliens, though the stations nearest to Earth on the tunnel network also have higher populations." She turned to her father, and for the first time in her life, addressed him by his first name. "Peter?"

"Yes, thank you, Mrs. Cohan," he replied facetiously. "The Stryx enforce very few regulations about commerce in and around their stations, most of these having to do with selling harmful substances such as banned Farling drugs, or weapons of mass destruction that they don't allow onboard in any case. They collect no taxes, but doing business on a station generally requires that you rent space, which always includes utilities. Wholesalers, which I imagine most of you to be, can operate directly out of their ships from rented docking space on the station core."

"How about middlemen?" somebody shouted out from the crowd.

"Do you have any middlemen on your world?" Peter shot back.

A loud "No!" was followed by another round of laughter.

"It's largely the same here," Peter continued. "Those of you who get a chance to visit Libbyland may wonder at the amount of underutilized space on Stryx stations, but the rents for warehousing goods are relatively high. The only distributors serving human businesses here deal in perishables, primarily food. Retail on the stations is split between high-rent boutiques and all-species market decks, which are patterned after the outdoor markets that are common throughout the galaxy."

"What would it take to get our goods into an auction?" another delegate called out.

"Bankruptcy," Shaina replied. She waited a long minute for the laughter to die down before continuing. "I don't know if any of you have had a reason to hold auctions on your worlds, but we deal almost exclusively in bankruptcies, sales of large estates, and occasionally in salvage from accidents involving cargo vessels. Most of the merchandise that would have gone to an auction house back on Earth gets snapped up by independent traders on the stations."

"Anybody else?" Kelly asked. She had taken the opportunity to read through a number of slips while Shaina was talking and was primed to go. "Next question, and this one is directly tied to what Mr. Doogal was speaking about earlier. Will the Thark insurance brokers on the stations underwrite contracts?"

This time it was the committee members who shared a laugh.

"The Thark bookies will underwrite anything," Stanley said. "You can bet on whether humanity will go to war with the Stryx, and if you want to bet on the humans to win, you'll get fantastic odds. But if you're looking for the Tharks to guarantee something less predictable than, say, goods lost to piracy, you'll find that they charge a stiff up-front fee for underwriting research before making the odds. They have limited experience dealing with humans, but if those of you living on Dollnick worlds are strictly following the Princely Standards, or applying the Consortium Scales on Drazen worlds, they might make you a good price."

"How about Verlock accounting?" a delegate called out.

"Quadruple entry bookkeeping?" Stanley appeared to be taken aback that any human would even consider the famously complicated system. "If you can figure out Verlock accounting, I expect you'll get a better rate from one of their Proof Funds than you'll get from the Tharks."

Kelly waited a moment before reading the next question. "Here's one that might be referring to the fact that the Galactic Free Press is distributed over the Stryxnet, though several of our panel members could comment. How did you get into business with the Stryx?"

"You start by asking," Chastity said, which drew a short laugh from the crowd. "I'm serious. The Stryx aren't a single entity and they all make their own decisions. The first generation Stryx, the ones who own and operate the stations, prefer to work in the background, but their offspring can be very active in business. Our station librarian participates directly in multiple human businesses, along with running several large enterprises of her own."

"One of the partners in our auction house is a young Stryx," Shaina added. "I can see him bobbing up and down over there and waving his pincer like he's waiting for a chance to say something, so perhaps we can expand the panel."

"I'm not sure…" Kelly started to say, but it was already too late. The Stryx drowned her out with a wailing siren, flashing lights on his casing like an old-fashioned emergency vehicle as he zipped up to where Kelly was standing. He gently nudged her out of the way.

"Thank you, Ambassador," Jeeves declared. He pirated her floating microphone, not because he needed it, but to keep her from objecting. "Thank you for inviting me, Shaina," he added, bobbing in his partner's direction. "So, I'd like to start by asking the person who submitted this question, do YOU have any money?"

The audience exploded in laughter at the Stryx's turning the tables on the questioner. All of the delegates were involved in business, either directly or indirectly, and they knew that humans had a reputation among the other species as being full of ideas and empty of pocket.

"Seriously, though," Jeeves continued. "If you look around at the advanced species, you'll find that very few of them invite the Stryx to participate in their businesses. Many of them are suspicious about our motivations, and for good reason. While we certainly don't object to making a profit, our first priority is always the protection of the tunnel network, which includes keeping the peace among our members."

"So you're saying if I want a partner for a weapons manufacturing plant, you aren't interested," remarked a man sitting right in front of the stage.

"Personally, I like weapons," Jeeves replied. "My main objection to joining a human business focused on military products is that from my standpoint, your technology is tens of millions of years out of date. But it's a valuable question because it highlights the limitations of Stryx participation in a non-Stryx business. Station librarians are generally happy to handle back-office work in their free time for a percentage of the gross, and younger Stryx such as myself may enjoy getting out and interacting with the inhabitants of the galaxy in a useful manner. But having a Stryx partner will not give you access to any technology or knowledge that can't be acquired through other means."

"We're out of time," Kelly whispered to Jeeves, who reluctantly allowed the microphone to float back to its rightful position. "I'm afraid that's all the time we have for questions," Kelly repeated, this time her voice going out to the crowd. "Our panel has volunteered to remain on the stage until lunch, and their contact information is included in the conference package, if you want to ping them later. Don't forget that the two-seat floater will be debuting on this stage at 3:00 PM today. Thank you for coming, and please let Junior Consul Cohan know if there's anything the embassy can do for you."

Nine

"I'm on my way now, but you could have given me a little more notice," Kelly grumbled at the ceiling of the lift tube capsule.

"I didn't want to distract you while you were moderating the panel discussion, and it would have been cruel to take you away before the free lunch EarthCent Intelligence sponsored. Besides, there's really nothing you need to prepare," Libby replied.

"I talked it over with the family and we decided to put the Cayl up in Ailia's old room. I'm taking your word for it that he's safe around children."

"The Cayl put their code of conduct before all else, and the obligations of a guest are rather extreme. While Brynt is staying in your home, he's honor-bound to treat you and your family the same way he treats his own flesh-and-blood."

"And how does this Brynt guy treat his own flesh-and-blood?" Kelly felt bad about questioning Libby's judgment, but over the years she'd discovered that it paid to read the fine print in alien codes of conduct.

"The same as you treat your own," Libby reassured her. "In addition, if you experience any difficulties during his stay, he will take them on as his own. Unscrupulous individuals from the member species of the Cayl Empire who are engaged in blood-feuds or experiencing business problems vie with one another to lure a Cayl as a guest. I hate to think of how many bankruptcies the Cayl have footed the bill for in the last few million years. A rigid code of conduct is a dangerous thing."

"So I take Brynt home first, since he represents the empire, and then I go back to escort the four emissaries to the embassies that are playing host?"

"They're all arriving together in a Cayl shuttle, making them Brynt's guests, so he'll expect you to take care of them before you pay attention to him."

"If you say so." Kelly stepped out of the lift tube into the main docking area and shifted to subvocing so passersby wouldn't think she was talking to herself. "And when will the shuttle be arriving?"

"Three. Two. One."

"That's a shuttle?" Kelly asked, as an alien ship gently came to rest on the deck just a hundred paces away. "You know I'm not that good with military stuff, but it looks more like a Horten destroyer than a simple transport."

"Looks can be deceiving," Libby replied. "It's more powerful than a Horten battleship. Don't forget that the Cayl created a military empire that includes thousands of star systems."

A section of the oversized shuttle's hull seemed to peel back as Kelly approached, and a platform bearing five passengers floated out of the opening and down to the deck. Kelly arrived just as the Cayl stepped off the platform, the four emissaries trailing respectfully at his heels.

"Welcome to Union Station," Kelly said, extending her hand to the Cayl, who wore a heavy gold chain around his neck. "You must be Brynt. I'm Kelly McAllister, the hostess for the Stryx open house."

"Kelly McAllister," the Cayl echoed her, getting the pronunciation correct.

Kelly was so surprised that she almost forgot to return his grasp when his hand wrapped around hers. The only one of her alien friends who could actually pronounce words in English was Dring. All of the others simply reproduced a facsimile of whatever their translation implants came up with, and without her own translation implant active, Kelly wouldn't have recognized their voices or known that they were addressing her. Her fingertips investigated the claws protruding from the back of the Cayl's hand, and he favored her with a smile, exposing an impressive set of canines.

"One of my duties as hostess is to take your emissaries around to the embassies of the tunnel network ambassadors they'll be living with and to make the introductions," Kelly said. "You'll be staying at my home, which is on this deck, so perhaps you'd prefer to wait in the shuttle and I'll return for you."

"Thank you for the consideration, but it is my responsibility to see these emissaries safely delivered to their temporary domiciles," Brynt replied politely. He turned to the four representatives of the dominant factions in the Cayl Empire and growled, "Introduce yourselves."

"But the creature already said that she's just a glorified guide," the most human-looking of the lot objected.

Kelly remembered what was behind the gold mask covering the Lood's face and said a silent prayer that he keep it on. She hadn't been thinking about third eyes when she ate far too much fruit salad with fresh grapes at the free luncheon, and suddenly her stomach felt queasy. Kelly couldn't see Brynt's response to the objection because his back was turned, but something in his demeanor must have sent the Lood a message.

"I am Z'bath," the masked humanoid pronounced coldly. He made no move to shake hands, which was fine by Kelly.

"Timba," said the alien who resembled an image of a Hindu god.

"Tarngol," grunted the silver-skinned Shuga, whose flat belly showed that he or she wasn't incubating an egg.

"Geed," the turtle-like creature declared. Kelly's translation implant gave the Tzvim's voice a friendly sound, and a decidedly female timbre.

"I'm pleased to meet you, Geed, Tarngol, Simba, Z'bath," Kelly replied.

"Timba," Libby whispered over Kelly's implant. The Nangor's trunk curled in disgust.

"I'm sorry, Timba," the ambassador corrected herself. "I see none of you are carrying luggage. Do you need a moment to return to the shuttle for your things before we get going?"

Four pairs of eyes stared at Kelly in disbelief, but Brynt silenced them with a low growl and turned back around to face their human host.

"It appears the traditions of our empire are somewhat different than those of the tunnel network," the Cayl explained mildly. "Our emissaries are entirely unused to manual labor of any form, and they expect all of their needs to be provided for by their hosts."

"I see," Kelly replied. She wondered if this was going to come as news to the Vergallians, the Grenouthians, the Hortens and the Dollnicks. "I suppose all that's left then is to get you settled in. Shall we?"

Kelly began walking backwards towards the lift tubes, feeling like a tour guide who had forgotten her script. After a dozen steps, when she was sure the group was following her, she turned around and completed the trip in silence. Upon entering the lift tube capsule, the EarthCent ambassador remained standing just inside the door, hoping that it would be interpreted as a gesture of respect.

As the aliens crowded together to enter the capsule, Kelly saw Timba's trunk brush the feathers of Tarngol's crest in the wrong direction, as if by accident. Z'bath gave the turtle-like Tzvim an unnecessary shove as she crossed the threshold, and the sharp-eyed Cayl delivered a kidney punch to the masked Lood's back. For a moment, Kelly was worried that she was going to be caught in the middle of a five-sided fight, but the Cayl growled and swatted the four emissaries to the points of the compass, with himself at the center.

"Vergallian embassy," Kelly told the ceiling. The sooner she was rid of the Lood the better.

"I presume I will be staying with the Vergallians," Timba said.

"You'll be staying with the Dollnicks," Kelly replied. "The Grenouthians are looking forward to hosting you, Geed, and the Hortens have been eagerly anticipating your arrival, Tarngol."

"Perhaps you didn't understand," Timba said icily. "As the senior emissary, I should be the first one introduced to my temporary quarters."

"Oh. We'll do it that way next time," Kelly replied as the door slid open. "The Vergallian embassy is just a few steps down the corridor, but you don't all have to come. Emissary Z'bath?"

101

Kelly extended her arm on a slight downwards angle, with the hand pointing more or less in the direction of the embassy, palm up. The Lood stepped out of the lift tube and strode off in the direction indicated, forcing the human ambassador to break into a jog to catch up. She glanced back at the lift tube and noted that the Cayl had herded the other emissaries out of the capsule, but was holding them back from following.

"It's just here," Kelly said, as they arrived in front of the Vergallian embassy. The ornate doors were closed, and even more surprisingly, failed to open automatically for the new arrivals.

"I see that Vergallian hospitality hasn't changed," the Lood stated in a bored voice. He pulled a small pouch from his sleeve, extracted a pinch of a green substance, and pushed it through the mouth-opening of his mask with a finger. "Perhaps I should have brought a locksmith."

"Libby?" Kelly subvoced. "Could you ping Aluria for me and find out what's going on?"

"She's trying to establish dominance," the Stryx librarian replied over the ambassador's implant. "Z'bath is aware of this and will no doubt do something to counter. You don't need to stay."

"If you don't mind waiting here, I should really get the other emissaries settled," Kelly said to the Lood. She felt terrible about leaving him standing in the corridor alone, but she trusted Libby's assessment and didn't see what would be accomplished by remaining.

Z'bath expertly spat a long stream of green juice at the doors of the Vergallian embassy, nodding his head and dropping his chin at the same time. Whatever was in the substance, Kelly was horrified to see that it solidified on contact, leaving something like a backwards "Z" scrawled across the entrance to the embassy. The doors slid open almost immediately after this act, and Aluria emerged, smiling sweetly.

"Emissary Z'bath, allow me to introduce you to Ambassador Aluria," Kelly stated formally. "I wish I could stay and chat, but the others are waiting." Then she beat a hasty retreat back to the lift tube, not wanting to see what the next phase of Lood-Vergallian maneuvering would bring.

The Cayl herded his three remaining charges back into the lift tube as Kelly approached. The moment she entered, the Nangor pronounced, "Dollnick embassy," and the capsule set off.

"You seem to be in a hurry today, Timba," the Shuga said conversationally.

"The early Nangor gets the Dollnick," Geed added, adroitly twisting to present her armored back when Timba pretended to lose his balance, causing his trunk to lash out in the direction of the Tzvim. Brynt intercepted the blow before it could land, and shoved the quarrelsome sentients further apart.

The rest of the brief ride passed peacefully and they arrived on the Dollnick deck, where the embassy was situated directly across from the lift tube. Crute was waiting in the corridor with a full panoply of liveried staff. Kelly stepped out of the capsule, the Nangor hard on her heels, and made the introduction.

"Emissary Timba, allow me to introduce you to Ambassador Crute."

Timba extended a hand, palm out, and for a moment, Kelly thought that he and the Dollnick were going to exchange a friendly greeting. When Crute's palm met Timba's, their fingers locked over each other, and then they both extended their other three arms the same way. As

Kelly ducked back into the lift tube, she could see the muscles of the four-armed alpha-males bulging, with each of them trying to force his counterpart to kneel.

"Watch out for his trunk," Brynt called a friendly warning to Crute.

"Horten embassy," the silvery Tarngol pronounced the moment the door closed, and the capsule set off smoothly. Neither of the two remaining emissaries nor the Cayl seemed the least bit surprised by the way the introductions were proceeding, so Kelly decided to bite her tongue and just get through it.

The Horten embassy was a short walk from the lift tube, and this time the Cayl and the Tzvim came along. Brynt expressed a favorable opinion of the station architecture as they strolled through one of the smaller commercial corridors. The skin response of the Horten residents who spotted the visitors reminded Kelly of the way a dance club mirror ball seemed to paint revelers different colors. In front of their embassy, the Hortens had prepared a reception similar to that of the Dollnicks.

"Emissary Tarngol, allow me to introduce you to Ambassador Ortha," Kelly declared.

Ortha responded with a mere head nod, and Tarngol barely ruffled the feathers on his crest.

"We'll just be going then," Kelly said, relieved that she wouldn't have to witness whatever animosity the alien diplomats held in store for each other. "I'll pick you up for the station tour tomorrow, Tarngol."

Receiving no reply, the ambassador led Geed and Brynt back to the lift tube. She had grown so accustomed to the emissaries of the Cayl Empire horning in on the navigation that she allowed five or ten seconds to tick by before asking the ceiling to take them to the Grenouthian embassy.

A double line of sash-wearing Grenouthians and the majority of the floating immersive cameras on Union Station met them when they exited on the most exclusive bunny deck. Kelly hadn't seen so many ranking Grenouthians in one place at one time since her first visit to their embassy.

"Emissary Geed, allow me to introduce you to, uh, the Grenouthian ambassador," Kelly said.

"Ambassador," Geed said politely.

"Emissary," the Grenouthian replied. He stepped forward, a scarlet sash held loosely in his paws. "Please allow me to present you with the pass to our warrens," he said formally.

Geed inclined her head and the Grenouthian ambassador arranged the sash over her shoulder. Although the Tzvim weren't as large as the bunnies, their natural armor gave their torsos surprising bulk, so the sash stopped mid-shell, rather than draping to her hip.

A band started to play and several reporters for the Grenouthian news networks hopped right up to the guest and began pelting her with questions. Kelly lost sight of the Tzvim as the large bunnies crowded around, and she retreated into the lift tube where the Cayl waited, a hand over the door to keep it from closing.

"Mac's Bones," she told the lift tube. "Well, so much for keeping your early arrival confidential, Brynt. Based on the number of reporters and immersive cameras I just saw, the Grenouthians are going to make this their lead story."

"By themselves, the emissaries are neither a threat nor particularly newsworthy," Brynt replied. "When the Stryx negotiated this exchange, I was impressed by their willingness to engage with such aggravating species. I hope there is plenty of security in place when the open house begins."

Kelly was still digesting this answer when they arrived back on the innermost deck, just down the corridor from Mac's Bones. She didn't remember the trip from the Grenouthian embassy being that short, but maybe Gryph had changed some of the routes.

"It's just this way," she encouraged the Cayl after they exited the capsule. "I didn't know you were involved in the open house negotiations. I'm afraid all I know about you, other than your name, is that you were sent along to accompany the emissaries."

"That's not exactly correct," Brynt told her. "It would be more accurate to say that the Stryx talked me into attending as an observer."

"So you represent the old Cayl leadership?" Kelly asked, trying to feel her way forward. Libby had made it sound like the Cayl had disbanded their empire in all but name and were merely acting as a paid mercenary force.

"I am the old Cayl leadership," Brynt told her casually as they entered Mac's Bones. "It's part of being emperor. And I can't tell you how much I've been looking forward to this trip. It's the first vacation from the empire I've ever taken."

The EarthCent ambassador almost fell over at Brynt's announcement. She was putting up the emperor of the Cayl Empire in Ailia's old room in their converted ice harvester? Kelly had told Joe that their guest would probably be a military functionary, a sort of a placeholder for the Cayl's honor. She was desperately subvocing Libby for a crash course on imperial etiquette when the sound of claws scratching frantically at the deck brought her attention back to what was happening right in front of her.

106

Beowulf skidded to an awkward halt, regarding the bear-like Cayl in puzzlement. The emperor seemed familiar somehow, despite being an alien of a sort the hound had never encountered. He heard Kelly shouting, "No, Beowulf. Down," and her body language suggested that she was overawed by their guest. So Beowulf dropped down low, his forelegs flat on the floor and his haunches up in the air, ready to move quickly as the situation warranted.

Kelly turned to apologize to Brynt for not warning him about their giant dog, but it was the Cayl emperor's turn to look surprised.

"Gurf?" Brynt asked, as if he couldn't believe his eyes.

Beowulf didn't know what a Gurf was, but he slapped his tail on the deck to demonstrate that he was disposed to treat any guest of the McAllisters like one of the family.

Brynt dropped to the deck, his forearms stretched out flat like Beowulf's forelegs, his own rear-end up in the air. Then he rose rapidly on all fours and galloped around to approach the dog in a flanking movement, before dropping back into the ready position.

Beowulf shifted the front of his body and gave a warning growl, and then he rose up and raced around in a circle, approaching the Cayl from behind. Before he got there, the Cayl was back up on all fours and sprinting away towards the training area, Beowulf in hot pursuit.

"Wait! Come back, Emperor!" Kelly shouted after the two racing quadrupeds, but neither of them paid attention. "Libby! Ping Joe and tell him the dog is fighting with the Cayl Emperor. Why didn't you tell me Brynt was the leader of one of the galaxy's military superpowers?"

"I didn't want to make you unnecessarily nervous," Libby replied soothingly. "He's really a very nice fellow."

"But why did he start chasing Beowulf?" Kelly demanded.

"Isn't it obvious?" the Stryx librarian replied. "They're playing."

Across the hold, Kelly heard somebody yelp, but she wasn't sure who.

Ten

"We've entered into orbit around the Cayl homeworld," Stryx Vrine informed the humans. "I used to have a pressurized observation deck set aside for biologicals, but I've mainly been off by myself the last few million years, so you'll have to make do with the hologram."

"The accommodations are great," Brinda said. "I never got the whole 'windows in space' concept anyway. Holograms are much more interesting."

"I see plenty of forests and mountains, but it could use some more oceans," Woojin observed. "Do we need to speak with the Cayl ground control, or are you handling all of the arrangements?"

"Young Jeeves completed the negotiations for this exchange before we left," Vrine replied. "The Cayl have already launched a transport to intercept my orbit and bring you to your temporary lodgings."

"That was fast," Brinda commented. "I wonder why they're giving us the VIP treatment?"

"The Cayl have been tracking my progress since I exited the temporary tunnel, and they supplied the course corrections for this parking orbit," Vrine explained. "In keeping with the Cayl's own tradition as both hosts and guests, I will comply with all reasonable requests and make myself available should they require assistance. They are among the most hospitable sentients in the galaxy."

"But it's a military empire, isn't it?" Lynx objected. "What are all those giant ships floating around above the planet in the hologram?"

"Warships, primarily," the Stryx said. "The Cayl home fleet is one of the largest combat forces maintained by biologicals in this galaxy. If they carry out their threat to wind down the empire, I plan to assign myself to this sector to observe the results."

"It's not a done deal?" Brinda sounded a bit disappointed. If the Cayl decided against liquidating their empire, there wouldn't be any need for the services of SBJ Auctioneers.

"The Cayl emperor has the final word, unless his people should replace him," Vrine replied. "I don't believe that's ever happened in the history of the Cayl Empire, but of course, the emperor has never dissolved the empire before. And without having been here to perform autopsies, I can't testify as to whether all of the previous emperors have died of natural causes."

"Will they understand us?" Lynx asked suddenly. "Libby updated our implants with the Cayl language, but we didn't bring any of those external voice boxes for speaking with aliens."

"Their technology is advanced well beyond any of the biological species you're familiar with from the tunnel network, and while they favor removable translation devices over surgical implants, I know that Jeeves supplied them with translation tables for English."

"How about food and air?" Brinda followed up. "They've never had human guests before, have they?"

"I don't imagine so," Vrine replied. "But the Cayl have been around for almost as long as I have, and they've long since perfected the synthesis technology required to meet the biological needs of alien species. All the same, I'm supplying you with a fresh set of diplomatic grade nose plugs to use if you venture outside and don't want to put your trust in their veil filters."

A cabin panel slid open and a bot carrying three sets of nose plugs entered. It also bore three necklaces with lockets for storing the plugs, which struck Lynx as overkill, since Union Station residents habitually wore their own. "I'll just pop the new plugs in my locket and leave the old ones with the bot," she said. "I'm used to the feel of this one."

"The new lockets double as communication devices should you wish to contact me," Vrine told her. "Your implants don't generate the power levels required to penetrate a full planetary atmosphere."

"They'd cook our brains if they did," Woojin said, taking a locket and a set of plugs. He removed his well-worn necklace and locket combo, handed it to the bot, and watched as Brinda and his wife did the same. "Will the Cayl transport extend a mating airlock, or will we be spacewalking through an extended atmosphere retention field?"

"Ah, they've just arrived," the Stryx announced. "Yes. I'll extend a field right up to their airlock. All you have to do is jump straight."

"I think I'm going to be sick," Lynx muttered.

A section of hull that formed the outer wall of their cabin retracted, leaving the humans staring out into the void. The boundaries of the atmosphere retention field were demarcated by subdued sparkling, where ionized particles from the solar wind contacted the invisible envelope.

A stubby, cylindrical vessel hung in space, seemingly motionless against a backdrop of stars. Its open airlock was outlined by blinking green lights, but it looked impossibly small to the humans.

"Will that airlock even fit the three of us, or are we going in one at a time?" Brinda asked.

"It only looks small because of the distance," the Stryx reassured them. "Cayl orbital regulations limit the closest approach between ships without standard empire-issued controllers to one percent of the length of the larger vessel. I am quite a large ship, and while the precaution is technically unnecessary in my case, traffic rules exist for a reason."

"This brings back memories," Woojin said, moving to the very edge of the surface that the humans had designated their floor in Zero-G. "It's just like the boarding drills we used to do, except without the armored spacesuits."

He bent his knees like a swimmer on a diving platform and used the anchor point of his magnetic cleats to pivot the rest of his body forward. Then he pushed off hard and floated in a straight line through the tunnel of air towards the Cayl transport. Somehow, he managed a slow somersault along the way and landed feet-first in the open airlock.

"Show-off!" Lynx shouted through the narrow passage of breathable air.

"I've reinforced the containment fields so you can't accidentally exit the pressurized corridor," Vrine said. When neither of the women made a move towards the opening, the Stryx added, "Would you like me to have the bot escort you?"

"Yes," Lynx and Brinda said simultaneously.

Once the three humans were reunited in the Cayl airlock, the bot returned to the science ship and tossed over their backpacks, which were fielded by Woojin with a series of "Oofs." The hatch closed after the transfer was complete, and there was a gentle hiss as the pressure equalized between the atmosphere in the airlock and the interior of the shuttle. The humans noticed a slight ozone smell, as if there had been a large electrical discharge on the ship.

"Thank you for traveling as my supercargo," Stryx Vrine said over their implants. "As long as I'm in the system, I'm going to go have a look at some of the local attractions, but I'll be back for you when the exchange is complete. The lockets will allow you to reach me at any time."

"Thank you," the three subvoced in reply. A moment later, the inner door of the airlock slid open.

"Welcome to the automated shuttle service owned and operated by Orbital Transports," a voice intoned. "Please follow the blinking lights in the deck to the passenger cabin and place yourself in an acceleration pod. You must stow your possessions in the space below your pod or in the secure locker at the front of the cabin. This transport cannot begin reentry until all safety precautions have been observed."

"Sounds reasonable," Woojin said, shuffling forward on his magnetic cleats. "Am I the only guy who wonders what we'll do if we ever encounter a species that builds spaceships out of aluminum?"

"What difference does it make?" Lynx demanded.

"Aluminum isn't ferromagnetic," Woojin explained. "Magnetic cleats won't work on it."

"Sure they will," Lynx argued. "I've been on lots of aluminum ships." She turned to Brinda for support, but the Hadad girl shook her head in the negative. "Anyway, let's get strapped in and down to the planet so we can eat some solid food, even if it is synthesized. Does anybody know what the gravity will be like?"

"A little less than we're used to," Brinda replied. "I asked Jeeves after he volunteered me to come along, and he said that the Cayl homeworld is a little larger than Earth, but it has less iron in the core."

"This see-through clamshell design reminds me of a Vergallian stasis coffin," Woojin said, after stowing his backpack in the compartment below the pod. "Looks like the lid is waiting to snap shut on us when we lie down."

"You're always in such a hurry to go first, so why don't you hop in and show us," Lynx said.

Woojin prodded the strange inner lining of the clamshell cover with a finger. The translucent material yielded easily, like a gel that was retained by little more than surface tension, and it released his finger without any suction.

"I wonder if we're supposed to remove our clothes before we get in these things," he said.

"No preparation is required before entering the pod," a voice informed them. "Continue to breathe normally when the cover closes. The gel is compatible with your respiratory system and will clear itself as a gas when you reach the planet's surface."

"That was more information that I wanted," the ex-mercenary remarked. He clicked his heels to turn off the magnetic cleats, and then used the pod's handholds to pull himself into the lower half of the clamshell, stretching out to his full length on the strange surface. Even in Zero-G, his body was pulled about halfway into the gel, like he was floating on his back in a very salty ocean. The top of the clamshell closed over him without a sound.

114

Lynx tapped on the cover, and Woojin turned his head towards her. He looked calm, and his lips moved like he was talking, but no sound came out.

"Are you still breathing?" Lynx subvoced over their private implant channel.

"I'm fine. Stow your stuff and hop in a pod so we can get moving."

"He says he's breathing," Lynx told Brinda, shoving her own backpack into the compartment beneath the pod next to her husband's. "I guess we may as well get it over with."

The two women entered their pods quickly, and as soon as the covers came down, they felt the slightest nudge of acceleration.

"How long do you think reentry will take?" Lynx subvoced.

"You're the pilot," Woojin replied in her head.

"The Stryx said that the Cayl are technologically more advanced than anybody we know from home, so that would include the Sharf and the Verlocks."

"Well, I know from experience that the Sharf make some disposable air-assault transports that can get a platoon from high orbit to the surface in a matter of minutes, but it's basically a controlled crash-landing."

"Have we even started down yet? I can't feel much of anything in this gel."

"Maybe it will be an unpowered reentry, and they're waiting for the right point in the orbit to fire braking rockets," Woojin speculated.

"I hope not. We could be in here for hours if that's the case."

"I don't think so. I got a decent look at the surface while I was flipping around between the science ship and the transport, and we're already in a very low orbit."

115

"How come we don't subvoc more often?" Lynx asked.

"Couples who subvoc together end up divorced," Woojin replied. "Too much intimacy or something."

"Did you feel that? Sort of like a lift tube capsule stopping. I think we're beginning reentry."

"I think my weight's back."

The clamshell lids of the three acceleration pods popped open and the humans looked at each other in surprise.

"Welcome to Cayl," the transport's voice announced. "We've set down at the imperial palace and I've informed them of your safe arrival. A welcome committee will be arriving to escort you to your destination. Thank you for traveling with Orbital Transports, and we hope to see you for your return trip."

"Did I miss something?" Brinda asked. A purple haze leaked out of her mouth and nose as she spoke. "I started reading a book on my heads-up display when the pod closed, and I only made it to page two."

"Whatever this gel is, I want some," Lynx said, observing her own purple breath. She swung her feet to the floor and stood up gingerly. "Look! No wobbles."

"It's all the traveling we've been doing lately," Woojin said. "You're getting your space legs back."

"How do we get out of this thing?" Brinda asked.

"Back the way we came?" Lynx suggested.

"We better put in the nose plugs the Stryx gave us," Woojin said, extracting his own from the locket.

The women followed suit and installed their own nose plugs, after which all three retrieved their backpacks from under the acceleration pods. Lynx led the way through the corridor to the airlock, the inner door of which had remained open. As soon as they all entered, the airlock cycled and the outer door dropped down, providing a shallow ramp to the tarmac.

"Does anybody see the welcoming committee?" Brinda asked when they reached the ground. The transport's ramp retracted and the ship leapt away from the surface, giving no sign of the propulsion system it was employing.

"Slick," Woojin said. "I wonder if it's a magnetic repulsion engine, or something with gravity. Oh, and I guess there's our welcoming committee. Isn't that a dog being chased by a bear?"

"He looks just like Beowulf," Lynx exclaimed, as the bounding dog drew nearer. Remembering how Joe's dog behaved when he was excited, she strategically moved behind Woojin.

A snow-white bear sprinted on all fours to catch the giant dog. When it became apparent that Beowulf's doppelganger was going to get to the humans first, the bear stopped short, stood up, and shouted, "No, Gurf! Down!"

Gurf skidded to a halt in front of the visitors, panting like he had just run around the entire planet. Up close, the humans saw that he was actually quite a few years older than Beowulf, and his eyes expressed a mournful disappointment at what he saw.

"I guess you were expecting somebody else," Woojin said, scratching behind the dog's ears. Gurf pressed against the human's hand, but he didn't contradict the statement.

"I'm sorry if he surprised you," the Cayl said, closing the remaining distance between them at a dignified walk. "You're the first hostages we've had in ages and I couldn't find a record for the protocol, but I'm sure we'll get along just fine without it. You'll have to forgive the mess, but it's been a madhouse since my husband announced his intention to dissolve the empire."

117

"Hostages?" Lynx asked.

"For my husband," the Cayl explained. "It wouldn't be fitting for him to leave the empire without a proper exchange of hostages. Didn't the Stryx tell you?"

"I guess Jeeves didn't think it was important," Brinda replied. "Uh, did you just say that you're the empress?"

"In the fur," the empress replied. "But you can call me Pava, everybody else does. We aren't much on formality."

"I'm Brinda Hadad," the auctioneer introduced herself, throwing in an awkward curtsey as an afterthought.

"Pyun Woojin and my wife Lynx," Woojin said.

"Are you a threesome?" Pava asked. "I don't know anything about your species beyond the reference information Stryx Jeeves sent, but I can arrange for a single room or connected suite if you alternate partners."

"I'd prefer a separate room for now," Brinda said, struggling not to laugh as Lynx glowered at her. "We're generally a pair-bonded species, though it varies with circumstances."

"Did that warship crash-land after losing a battle?" Woojin asked, pointing at the hulk of an immense vessel that loomed over the edge of the tarmac.

"That's the imperial palace," Pava replied apologetically. "It was in fact the flagship of the home fleet a very long time ago, but a combination of age and combat damage necessitated its replacement. The emperor at that time was so attached to the ship that he brought it down to serve as his residence, and living there has turned into one of those family traditions that grow up over the years. It's a bit embarrassing when we have guests."

"Hostages," Lynx muttered under her breath.

"Hostages are especially honored guests," the empress replied, blissfully unaware that the human had expected the comment to go unheard. "It works both ways, you know. You can think of my husband as being hostage for our good treatment of you."

"Gurf here misses the emperor?" Woojin asked.

"The two of them have been inseparable since the hound was a puppy, but Brynt heard that he'd be staying with an ambassador's family and didn't want to impose. Gurf's been moping around ever since my husband departed, though I'll have to say it hasn't affected his appetite."

"Brynt?"

"Emperor Brynt," Pava said, without a hint of condescension. She began leading the humans back to the wreck that served as the imperial palace, talking all the while. "The whole business with titles and bloodlines is very old-fashioned, but we Cayl decided long ago that somebody had to be in charge. The alpha-male of Brynt's line drew the short straw some ten thousand generations ago."

"The same family has ruled for ten thousand generations?" Lynx asked.

"They've tried abdicating, of course. At least ten thousand times, but the rest of the Cayl were having none of it. My mother cried like a lost Skreelink when I told her I was marrying Brynt, but he chased me so hard that I couldn't help myself. I do hope the Stryx choice for a host is treating him well."

"He's staying with the ambassador for our species, the humans," Brinda said. "They live in the crew quarters of an old interstellar ice harvester that's permanently parked in one of Union Station's holds, so the Emperor should feel right at home."

"That's wonderful." Pava sounded genuinely relieved. "The Dowager Empress has been at me about not accompanying her son ever since he left, but I'm babysitting all of the cubs in the family while their parents are running around the empire visiting garrisons to reassure the warriors. The truth is, Brynt left things in a bit of an uproar, but his mother thinks he's perfect," she added, rolling her eyes. "I'll deliver you to her after you get a chance to rest up."

"Is she the official hostage keeper?" Woojin asked.

"Yes, but I'm in charge of feeding you," the empress said. "The Dowager Empress wanted to hold the meal immediately after you arrived, but I explained that you'd be tired from traveling and that I'd need some time to study up on your biology to synthesize a decent meal. Nutrition is easy, but before I took over the kitchen, our alien guests used to complain that everything tasted like wet dog fur." A steady rain began to fall on the group before they made it halfway to the palace wreck. "Of course, it does rain here every afternoon, and the dogs do like shaking themselves off indoors."

Eleven

Joe looked up from reading a service manual when his father-in-law returned. "So what did you think of the fishing, Steve? Worth the trip from Earth?"

"They looked kind of like overgrown goldfish," the old man replied, easing himself into one of the patio chairs. "The truth is, Marge gets restless sitting around the house counting her money, but she worries that I'm not in good enough shape to travel. So I try to guess where she wants to go, and then I insist we make the trip. Did you really think I spent five days in stasis on that ship because I wanted to go fishing on Union Station? Still, if that park is your idea of a sewer plant, this is a pretty sweet spot you're living in."

"Sorry I couldn't go along with you and Samuel this time," Joe said. "It's just me and Thomas running the training camp while Woojin and Lynx are visiting the Cayl Empire. I don't think you ever met them, Steve, but I've known Woojin longer than I've been married to your daughter."

"So where are our girls?" Steve asked. Samuel stared at his grandfather, round-eyed. That anybody could refer to his mother or grandmother as girls was beyond the nine-year-old's comprehension.

"Kelly's out with Brynt on another round of embassy visits and Dorothy is at work," Paul answered. He set

121

down a tray with two glasses of Joe's latest microbrew, a small bottle of prune juice, and an apple for Samuel. "Marge went with Aisha to the studio to watch her shoot the show, and they took Fenna with them, even though she sleeps through it."

"I sure feel bad drinking beer in front of you like this," Joe said to his father-in-law.

"I gave up beer at eighty, wine at eighty-five, and I'll give up Scotch at ninety if I make it that long," Kelly's father replied. "But I only drink the Scotch at night, after Marge goes to bed."

"Why's that, Grandpa?" Samuel asked.

"So she doesn't see me," the old man replied. "But don't tell her. It's a secret."

Beowulf scrabbled out from under the table and loped off towards the entrance of Mac's Bones.

"Somebody new must be coming," Samuel said through a mouth full of apple. He made a mighty effort to swallow, and then he set out after the dog.

"Pretty efficient alarm system you have there." Steve took a sip of his prune juice and coughed. "I don't want you boys to think that I'm more senile than Marge makes me out to be, but I'm still a little confused about the whole dog situation. You started with some sort of genetically engineered cross between an Earth mutt and a Huravian hound, that dog died, but then he came back as a full-blooded Huravian?"

"That's right," Joe said. "And now we've learned that the Huravian hounds aren't native to Huravia. I knew the Huravian monks claimed to be an ancient military order, and apparently they were trained by early Cayl explorers who left them some dogs. I asked Dring to join us this evening and we'll find out if he knows anything about it."

Samuel returned to the patio area in front of the ice harvester and breathlessly reported, "It's a big kid. He must have food or something because Beowulf is walking back with him."

"Maybe I'll bring up a pitcher and another Libbyland glass," Joe said. "Does anybody else want something?"

"Aisha was saving a coconut curry for Dring," Paul said. "It's one of the few cooked dishes he likes, but don't heat it up."

As Joe got up and headed off on his errand, Beowulf broke away from the approaching visitor and streaked off in the direction of the training grounds.

"He only runs that fast for one of us or for Brynt," Samuel observed.

"Must be Dring coming," Paul agreed.

Kelly's father chuckled.

"What's funny, Grandpa?" Samuel asked.

"You know, I've only been off of Earth three times in my life, and all three were to see my daughter and her family. I can't get over how you boys talk to all of these aliens just like they're humans, even Dring, that clone friend of Dorothy's, and this Cayl fellow who's visiting. If I saw any of them coming my way in a dark alley on Earth, I'd run the other direction."

"You shouldn't run," Samuel said, taking his grandfather literally. "Mommy told me I shouldn't even make you walk fast."

"Hello?" the newcomer called as he approached within earshot of the seated group. "Is this the McAllister residence?"

"Yes it is," Paul replied. "The chief of the clan is getting you a beer, providing you pass the beard test. Were you looking for a place to park the family ship?"

"What? No, I don't have a family, or a ship," the kid replied. "I came to talk to Dorothy's father."

"Well, I'm her grandfather, young fellow, and these two are her brothers, so I hope your intentions are honorable," Steve said, doing his best to look stern.

"Yes, sir," the boy replied, turning a dull shade of red. "My name is David Coughlin, I think, and I..."

"Hold on a minute," the old man interrupted. "You better wait for her father to come back so you don't have to repeat yourself, unless you wanted to practice a bit first. You sounded pretty unsure about your name, there."

"What's in the box?" Samuel asked.

"Oh," David said, looking down at his hands. "I asked Mr. Ainsley what I could bring to make a good impression, and he said that your family likes leftovers. Then Mrs. Ainsley waved a kitchen knife at him and she gave me this. It seems heavy for a cake."

Joe emerged from the ice harvester with a pitcher of beer, another glass, and a casserole dish of coconut curry. The Maker and Beowulf timed their arrival perfectly, and the dog immediately shifted his attention back to the white box held by the young man.

"Thanks for coming, Dring," Joe said. "We seem to be having a males-only party this evening."

"I'm honored to be invited," Dring replied politely, taking care to position himself between Paul and Kelly's father, so as not to scare the stranger. "I don't recall meeting this young man before."

"He's David something, and he's here to complain about Dorothy," Samuel said.

"No, you didn't understand," David protested, his face turning a brighter shade of red. "I wanted to, uh, ask about her."

124

Joe reached the table, looked the boy up and down, and then turned towards Beowulf to get his opinion of the stranger. The dog was staring in rapt concentration at the white box from Pub Haggis and missed the unspoken request.

"You look old enough for a beer, so don't say no," Joe said, pouring out a glass from the pitcher and handing it to the boy across the table. "Somebody open up that box before Beowulf decides to swallow the whole thing."

David set the box on the table, and as the resident expert at Pub Haggis deliveries, Samuel undid the cover flap and flattened out the sides. A deep glass dish with a brown crust was revealed, and the rich smell of shepherd's pie invaded willing nostrils.

"Why don't you two get some plates and silverware," Joe said, nodding to Paul and Samuel.

"Sir?" David asked in trepidation, as soon as the younger McAllisters entered the ice harvester.

"Will it spoil your appetite to wait until after we eat?" Joe replied in irritation.

"Yes, sir,"

"What's on your mind, David Something?" Joe asked in resignation. He'd been hoping that this particular scene wouldn't play out until Dorothy was at least twenty, but she was already as tall as her mother and better educated than he'd ever be.

"Coughlin, sir. I think. I want your permission to ask your daughter to go on the Physics Ride with me. It's the new..."

"I know what it is," Joe cut the boy off abruptly. "I'm down there every other day fixing the damn steam organ. Have you talked to Dorothy about going to Libbyland together?"

"No, sir. I don't know much about how to act around family people, but Dorothy explained that on the station, I could ask the Stryx librarian for help about anything."

"Libby sent you to ask me whether you can take my sixteen-year-old daughter on a date?"

"Yes, sir. I mean, not a date, sir. But Dorothy has helped me so much, and I want to do something for her."

"Quick, before the boy gets back. Where did you come from and why aren't you sure about your last name?"

"I don't remember anything before being cabin boy on a small trader with Coughlin. He said he was my father, but I think that might have been a lie. When I started growing and asking questions, he indentured me to a mining outfit as a powder monkey. I stowed away on a Gem tramp freighter three months ago and ended up here."

"Powder monkey," Joe repeated. "You mean they sent you in the narrow tunnels with a laser drill to set charges."

"Yes, sir."

"What do you think, Dad?" Joe asked his father-in-law.

"When Kelly was that age, she was too busy reading about boys in books to meet any. We were pretty worried about her until you came along."

"All right, David. Sit down, drink your beer and stay for dinner. But if you make her cry, I'll find you and feed you to the dog."

"Thank you, sir," David said. He started breathing normally again and settled awkwardly into a patio chair.

The two younger McAllister males chose that moment to start down the ramp, confirming Dring's suspicion that Paul had been holding Samuel back from returning while Joe interviewed the young man. The whole scene fit nicely into the Victorian novels Dring was fond of borrowing from Kelly, and he felt privileged to have witnessed the human ritual of vetting Dorothy's first suitor.

"Kelly pinged me to ask what we were doing for dinner," Paul said, while Samuel noisily dealt the plates as if they were playing cards. "She's stuck at a Verlock reception with Brynt and she says they won't be home until late."

"Fine fellow, the Cayl emperor," Dring commented. "Oldest dynastic bloodline in the galaxy, to the best of my knowledge. I met several of his ancestors on my last surf through that part of space."

"Did you see any Huravian hounds while you were there?" Paul asked. He handed around silverware, wrapped in cloth napkins like the utensils at a catered event.

"The Cayl hounds weren't all quite as large as Beowulf, but that's just a matter of gravity, environment, and natural selection playing out over a couple of million years," Dring replied. "Just as smart, though.

Beowulf looked away from the shepherd's pie long enough to acknowledge the indirect compliment with a lolling tongue.

"Why didn't you ever mention it?" Paul asked.

Dring took a forkful of cold coconut curry and chewed slowly before answering. "You know, it's statistically implausible that so many sentient species of widely varying forms and biology are blessed with companions that not only fill the role that dogs played in Earth's history, but are outwardly similar in form."

"What's he mean?" Samuel and his grandfather asked Paul at the same time.

"Xenobiologists take it for granted that somebody subtly altered the genes of predecessor species on worlds all over the galaxy to produce something like dogs," Paul explained.

"And what's HE mean?" Samuel asked his father.

"You've heard of Stryx science ships, haven't you?" Joe inquired. Samuel nodded. "The aliens don't consider it a fit topic for conversation, but the general feeling is that the Stryx do more than just observe. Some scientists think they interfere to help civilizations develop, and it could be that making sure everybody gets a dog is at the top of the list."

"Except the Grenouthians," Samuel commented. "Dogs chase bunnies."

Paul and Dring kept up a conversation about dogs and space travel as they ate, with frequent interruptions from Samuel. But Joe was uncharacteristically uncommunicative, and David barely said a word throughout the meal.

When the food was gone and the pitcher of beer was empty, Joe instructed Samuel, "Wake up your grandfather and help him get to his room." As soon as the boy and the old man were up the ramp, he turned to his daughter's admirer. "Put that casserole dish down for the dog and he'll save you the trouble of cleaning it."

Beowulf perked up as the boy put the shepherd's pie container on the deck. The dog calculated that through strategic begging and licking off the individual plates as they became available, he had already eaten more of the pie than any of the humans, but the crunchy bits left in the baking dish were his favorite part.

"Dorothy won't be home from work for another two hours if you were waiting," Joe said.

"No, sir. I knew she was at work. I just came to talk to you."

"So the two of you have already been seeing each other."

"No, sir. I mean, after she got me the job at Pub Haggis, she comes to check on me sometimes when she gets out of work, so I sort of know her schedule. I think she wants to make sure I don't embarrass her with the Ainsleys."

"I'm sure that's it," Joe snorted, wondering what his daughter saw in the gangly boy. Maybe Kelly would be able to explain it. "Well, thank you for coming to ask. If Dorothy agrees to go anywhere with you, I expect you to come here to meet her mother."

"Yes, sir," the boy said, taking it as a dismissal. He rose to go, retrieving the sparkling casserole dish from the floor.

"Don't waste your money renting gear for the Physics Ride," Paul added. "The suit rental clerks know Dorothy if I'm not there. If she didn't mention it already, I'm sort of the Libbyland engineer."

David headed home to his temporary lodgings, and Joe busied himself studying the translated Sharf engine-rebuild manual on his tab while he waited for his wife to get home.

Inside the ice harvester, Kelly's father said to Samuel, "Remember not to tell Grandma about the Scotch."

"I have a secret too," Samuel told his grandfather shyly.

"You can tell me," the old man said. "That will make it even."

"You promise, cross your heart and hope to be turned into a Horten?"

"Cross my heart and hope to be turned into a Horten."

"I have to show you," Samuel said. "It's in my room."

The boy led his grandfather through the crew quarters of the converted ice harvester to his own unique space, which had once contained all of the field generation equipment for the ice sweeps.

"Beowulf, Banger and Jeeves are the only other people I let in here," the nine-year-old told his grandfather earnestly. "Well, Mommy sticks her head in sometimes, but only if I'm being really quiet."

"That makes sense," the old man replied seriously.

"It may not work right now. It depends on whether she's home and what time it is there," Samuel added, as if he was afraid he might disappoint his grandfather's expectations. The boy took his robot souvenir from Libbyland off of its special shelf and set it on the floor. Next he picked up the remote and touched a number of symbols. The little robot's eyes lit up with an emerald green glow, and a hologram of the other little robot from the Libbyland gift shop appeared right in front of it.

"She's there," Samuel declared joyfully, and then shifted to speaking Vergallian, "Ailia?"

"Hi, Samuel." The response seemed to come out of the robot hologram's mouth. "You're early today."

"What did it say?" Kelly's father asked.

"I forgot you don't have an implant," Samuel said. "Ailia. My grandfather is here and he promised to keep our secret. Can we talk in English today, and then we'll do two times of Vergallian in a row?"

"Okay," the little voice came out of the hologram of Ailia's robot. "Have you started taking dance lessons like you promised?"

"I'm still practicing with Banger," Samuel mumbled. "I know he doesn't have arms or legs, but he uses a holothing to teach me."

"You need to dance with a real girl," Ailia said with authority. "Baylit invites a different boy to practice with me every week. She says it's important to honor their families, and that one of the most important skills I can learn as queen is how to dance with clumsy oafs without getting my toes crushed."

"You're talking with that little Vergallian girl who went back to her home?" Samuel's grandfather asked in wonder. "How is that possible?"

"Jeeves made our robots to show how the toys would look, but he used Stryx ship controllers to make them work," Samuel related excitedly. "Banger says they connect the same way as the Stryxnet, but because Jeeves made them as a pair, it's all direct and it doesn't cost us anything. They're pro-types."

"Prototypes," his grandfather guessed.

"Oh, my lady-in-waiting is coming. I have to go," the hologram of Ailia's robot said hurriedly. "See you later." The hologram winked out.

"That's some secret," Kelly's father said, rubbing his chin thoughtfully. "I guess we're even. Are you going to sign up for dance lessons?"

"I have to," Samuel groaned. "Don't want to turn into a Horten."

Twelve

"I thought that the five of you might be interested in seeing how humans are adapting to the tunnel network," Kelly said, though she suspected that Brynt was the only alien in the group paying attention. After several days of playing tour guide, she had grown used to walking backwards while being ignored by the emissaries from the Cayl Empire.

"Why do you think the Stryx are so keen on showing us the lower classes?" the Lood emissary remarked loudly to the others, as if Kelly wasn't there. "Are they trying to tempt us by showing how easily we could dominate these species?"

"Who would want to?" the Nangor replied. "When my Dollnick host told me that they allow these Human creatures to settle on their open worlds, I laughed so hard that I began to choke and had to perform the Glurisch maneuver on myself."

"Both of you behave," the Cayl emperor barked, throwing in a few lightning jabs to make his point. "Please continue, Ambassador McAllister."

"The trade show we're about to enter is associated with the Third Annual Conference of Sovereign Human Communities. More than a third of the representatives are attending from the open Dollnick worlds you were referring to, Emissary Simba."

"Timba," Libby reminded Kelly over her implant.

"I know," Kelly subvoced in reply.

"So these communities you are referring to are under the authority of your EarthCent government?" Emissary Geed asked politely.

"Oh, no," Kelly replied. "EarthCent isn't really a government, except in the sense that the humans spread around the tunnel network don't have anything else. The conference represents an effort on the part of these communities to find common ground and potentially evolve in the direction of a representative assembly."

"So it's true what the Horten told me, that you're all Stryx welfare cases," Tarngol said. The Cayl responded with a threatening look, and the silvery alien decided that he needn't repeat the rest of the Horten's analysis.

"As a Stryx protectorate, Earth is off-limits for armed invaders from other species, and all tunnel network members living on stations benefit from the same protections," Kelly answered smoothly. "The humans you'll meet today are living on alien worlds and don't have a direct relationship with the Stryx, other than buying some communications services. But as those worlds are also part of the tunnel network, they fall under the same Stryx rules that prevent member species from warring on one another."

"And what about attacks from off-network species?" Brynt asked.

"If any of the advanced species want help defending one of their worlds, my understanding is that the Stryx will intervene on request. But after stopping the war, they will judge the cause and assign reparations."

"You mean, if we became part of the tunnel network and some foreign species attacked one of our worlds, the

133

Stryx might side with the aggressors after stepping in to end the fighting?" Z'bath asked in amazement. It was the first time he had addressed the EarthCent ambassador without being prompted to do so by Brynt.

"If you were at fault," Kelly replied. "It's not an area where I have any experience, but I've heard stories from other ambassadors. Suppose you had, uh, taken something from an off-network species without permission, like a world they had been terraforming, and then that species sent a fleet to demand compensation. Would it be fair to expect the Stryx to destroy them so that you could keep what you, er, took?"

The Lood came to an abrupt halt. He stared at the EarthCent ambassador, and she could almost feel his third eye boring in on her, even though it was concealed behind the golden mask. The three other emissaries appeared to be equally stunned, and even Brynt's expression showed puzzlement.

"Tell me again," Z'bath said. "Why exactly would we want to join this tunnel network?"

"My understanding is that the Cayl are stepping down as your protectors and the rest of you don't get along well enough to be trusted with warships," Kelly replied sharply. The Lood had a way of exhausting her diplomatic reserves in a hurry. "Of course, if you want to spend all of your money and resources building up fleets and destroying each other, that's your affair."

"Is this flexibility to assign reparations included in the contract that the Stryx and the tunnel network members sign?" the Cayl inquired carefully.

Kelly glanced around guiltily before replying, feeling ridiculous all the while, since Libby was clearly listening in over her implant. "The Stryx tend to reserve the right to do whatever they think is best in all of their contracts, even the simple leases for station real estate. There's a legal term for it that I'm forgetting."

"Divine right?" Geed suggested.

"You make the tunnel network sound so attractive," Timba added sarcastically.

"Anyway, let's put this discussion on hold and go inside," Kelly said. "I'm aware that the goods at this trade show are unlikely to meet your standards, but the people displaying them worked hard to get this far, so I hope you treat them as you would your own citizens."

"Don't even think about it," Brynt growled at the emissaries. "Treat them like you would treat me."

"Thank you, Emperor," Kelly said, belatedly realizing her mistake.

The ambassador was beginning to feel sorry for the Cayl and sympathized with him for wanting to be rid of such a fractious empire. She led the group through the lower entrance to the Galaxy room, which opened into the trade-show area beneath the seats. The four emissaries kept a curb on their usually derisive commentary for almost an entire minute before the group reached the first booth, a display of textiles from Chianga.

"Look," exclaimed the Shuga, barely able to contain his mirth. "Textiles made from plant fiber. Have you ever seen anything so quaint?"

"I'll bet the manufacturing process includes chewing," Timba added. "And they probably color the fabric with dyes made from bodily effluents."

"Actually, the clothes I'm wearing now are made from plant fibers, cotton to be precise, and early humans used stale urine to bind natural dyes to fabrics," Kelly said combatively. The Cayl gave her a nod of approval. "I believe the textiles on display here are actually produced using a Dollnick process, Timba, so perhaps you'd like to save your observations for Ambassador Crute."

"Isn't that Yttrium?" muttered Z'bath, peering through the crowd at a hologram of an atom floating above a booth. "I make it thirty-nine protons, but I can't be certain with this foolish mask."

"Thirty-nine it is," Brynt confirmed. "I'm warning you, though. Don't cause a scene."

"I just want to see what they're selling it for," the Lood said, setting off for the booth. Kelly and the Cayl stayed with him, but the three other emissaries followed at a leisurely pace, commenting to each other on the human products as if they were museum installations.

"How much for the Yttrium?" Z'bath demanded of the human behind the table.

The man looked back at the Lood blankly. Either he didn't have an implant or it didn't include languages from species that weren't local.

"He'd like to know what you charge for Yttrium," Kelly interpreted.

"We don't have any for sale," the man replied. "All of our production goes to the Drazens as part of our deal with the Two Mountains consortium."

"Then why is the fool advertising it?" Z'bath demanded.

Kelly translated again, leaving out the slur, and the man replied, "It's not an advertisement. It's the logo of our mining consortium. I see the gentleman is partial to gold accoutrements. Shall I check the spot price for him?"

The Lood shook his head in disgust and stalked back towards the other emissaries, the Cayl staying by his side.

136

"I'm sorry," Kelly apologized to the salesman. "He's not from around here."

"Let's keep it that way, shall we?" the man replied.

When Kelly caught up with the group, the Cayl was herding them towards one of the short access tunnels that connected with the center stage of the Galaxy room. "Did I miss something?" she asked Brynt.

"Geed discovered that a manufacturer is showing a small ground transport of the floating variety," the emperor replied. "She collects such vehicles, as do the other emissaries. It's a popular way of displaying status without amassing wealth, since they depreciate so quickly."

"You must be talking about the Chiangan floater based on the Dollnick design," Kelly replied. "I've heard about it, though I missed the unveiling when you arrived. But why do the emissaries want to avoid getting rich?"

"My ancestors discovered in the early days of our empire that wealth had an unhappy tendency to concentrate under all of the native political systems we found ourselves supervising. To prevent this from happening to the extent that it destabilizes society, we put in place a special wealth tax on all of the member planets. Every Cayl year, the wealthiest person on each world must deliver half of their assets to a planetary beautification fund."

"How does a special tax on just one individual per planet change anything?" Kelly asked.

"It changes mindsets," Brynt replied. "The citizens of the Cayl Empire still chase after wealth and comfort, but nobody wants to be the richest. Charitable giving across the Empire always peaks before the annual assessment, as the individuals who worry they might come out at the top of the list maneuver for a lower seeding."

"But don't they cheat by making local laws that let them hide money in different ways?"

"The Cayl don't allow cheating," Timba said sullenly. "They have no respect for creative solutions."

"Don't let the fur and the fangs trick you," Z'bath added. "Every year a greedy fool on some world or another thinks he can outsmart the Cayl inspectors, and instead of losing half of his fortune, he loses the whole thing."

"All of the worlds in the Empire have very nice parks," Geed added.

Kelly and her group emerged from the tunnel onto the center stage of the Galaxy room, where a two-seater version of a standard Chiangan floater was just coming to rest. It was driven by a girl who couldn't have been much more than ten years old. A man, assumedly her father, broke off his sales pitch to an audience of convention delegates as the diplomats approached.

"Bob Winder," he introduced himself to Kelly. "I'm the mayor of Floaters and I've been hoping for a chance to tell you how much I enjoyed your panel discussion. I spoke with Marge Frank about visiting Earth to raise investment capital and I think I might risk it."

"Risk?" Kelly said. "I can personally vouch for Mrs. Frank. To tell you the truth, she's my mother."

"Family business, eh?" the mayor said, giving her an exaggerated wink. "Same here, that's my daughter Sephia demonstrating the floater. Let's get you introduced."

The young girl exited the floater by stepping over the low gunwales and skipped over to her father.

"Can I go again, Daddy?" she asked. "It's so much fun driving in here with all the giant steps."

"They're seats," her father told her. "It's just the way some species build amphitheatres."

"Not very Dollnick," his daughter observed dismissively.

"Hi," Kelly said, offering the girl her hand. "I'm Ambassador Kelly McAllister, and these sentients are guests from the Cayl Empire. Apparently they're all vehicle collectors, and they've expressed an interest in your floater."

"Well, I'll be happy to tell you about it," Bob said. "We've been producing floaters from Dollnick components on Chianga for years, and we recently licensed the right to create a two-seater sports version based on our own design. It's still Dollnick technology, and the performance boost comes from using the same drive unit that powers — Hey, where do you think you're going?"

Kelly followed the mayor's eyes and saw that the floater was racing away, the Shuga at the controls. Brynt cursed and dropped to all fours, sprinting after the floater, which barely cleared the lip of the first row of faux-stone benches. The craft was designed to float close to the ground, and while it could handle reasonable bumps, driving straight into vertical blocks while accelerating was risky business.

"What's that alien doing?" Bob demanded of Kelly. "Trying to steal a floater on a space station?"

Incredibly, Brynt was gaining on the floater, bounding upwards three tiers at a time, when Tarngol threw it into a sudden turn. The craft tilted to a forty-five-degree angle as it took its ground reference from two rows of stepped benches. The floater gained speed as soon as it stopped climbing, and the Cayl's attempt to cut the angle and leap aboard missed by a hair. The emperor crashed into a seating tier, but he got back on his feet immediately and began climbing higher.

"It can't get in a wreck, can it?" Kelly asked anxiously. "I'm sure you must build them with anti-collision systems and such."

"If that nut who's driving gets it up to top speed in here, something has to give," Bob replied grimly. "The seating in this room is banked like a racetrack, if you hadn't noticed."

"What's the bear-guy doing?" Sephia asked excitedly.

Kelly looked up and saw that the Cayl emperor was back on all fours, racing along the seating tier a little higher up than the Shuga was driving. As the floater went into its second lap around the room, still gaining speed, Brynt leapt in the air. Kelly was sure he had miscalculated and the vehicle would hit him dead on, but instead he landed hard, half on the empty seat and half on the Shuga. The sudden weight increase almost flipped the floater, but it recovered, and the emergency program brought it to a rapid halt.

Kelly feared for the worse as she led the charge up the stairs, moving like she was twenty years younger. She couldn't help wondering why the Stryx hadn't interfered, grabbing the floater with a manipulator field or shutting it down remotely. When she reached the hovering vehicle, she saw why no help had been necessary.

Brynt was helping the shaken Shuga to his feet, and even brushed a hand over the alien's crest to settle his ruffled feathers. At the same time, he was lecturing Tarngol on his manners.

"What did I tell you about how to treat the Humans?"

"But it's not a Human, it's a machine," the Shuga protested. "Anyway, with the top open like this, I was sure it would have some kind of field to keep you from jumping in."

140

"It's a recreational vehicle," the emperor replied. "The force field is to keep out the wind and the rain, maybe protect the occupants against an accidental bird strike. You thought it would stop a Cayl warrior?"

"I guess I didn't think," Tarngol admitted sulkily, then winced when he stepped down a row.

"I might have cracked one of your ribs with that landing," Brynt said. "If I was a few hundred years younger, I could have matched speeds with the floater and it would have gone easier on you."

Bob leaned into the vehicle and pressed a button.

"Running full self-diagnostic," the floater announced. "Structural integrity, pass. Drive unit, pass. Levitation, pass. Field generator, overload. Degaussing. Retuning crystals. Field generator restart. Diagnostic retest. Field generator, pass."

"Well, no serious harm done, I guess," Bob said, shaking his head at the aliens. "You'll forgive me if I don't invite any of your other guests to try it," he added, for Kelly's benefit.

"No, of course. I think we've had enough driving for one day," Kelly replied hastily.

"How much does one of these cost?" Geed asked. "I was favorably impressed with its ease of operation and survivability."

"The sticker price is twenty thousand Stryx cred," Bob replied after Kelly translated. He eyed the Tzvim speculatively.

"Do you offer a diplomatic discount?" Geed inquired.

Kelly translated and the salesman replied, "For recognized diplomats."

"I'm traveling incognito until the start of the open house," the Tzvim said. "Would you vouch for me, Ambassador?"

"The Tzvim really is a diplomat, but we're trying to keep things quiet until the Stryx open house officially begins," Kelly explained.

"I'll believe it when I read it in the Galactic Free Press," Bob said stubbornly. He climbed into the floater and began easing it back down towards the central stage. "If you do qualify, the diplomatic discount is five hundred creds," he called back over his shoulder.

"That's not even three percent," Geed complained. "In our empire, senior diplomats get thirty percent off on durable goods and fifty percent off on meals and entertainment."

"Your empire?" the Cayl inquired dryly.

"We aren't the ones stepping down," Z'bath pointed out.

Thirteen

"It's really not about the money," Kelly reassured the Cayl emperor, who stood behind the EarthCent ambassador to observe her play. "It's a game of strategy and chance. The chips are just a way of keeping score."

"We don't disapprove of gambling," Brynt replied. "It's the pursuit of wealth that we find destructive."

"You mean you gamble to lose?" Joe asked. A smile spread over his face. "Kelly. Why don't you swap places and we'll teach Emperor Brynt how to play."

"No objections here," Daniel said. "Or, you could just have him pull up a chair and we'll stick with games that allow more than eight players."

"I've invented a new game that allows up to thirteen players using just one standard deck," Jeeves announced. "It's like five-card stud, except with four cards, and everybody gets an invisible wildcard."

"What do you call it?" Dring asked, shuffling with his stubby fingers.

"Jeeves," the Stryx replied. "It's my back-up plan for immortality."

"Sorry, Jeeves, but I've seen it played in casinos," Daniel said. "And I haven't had a chance to thank you for helping out with the conference panel, so, thank you."

"Aisha is looking after the baby," Shaina told her husband as she retook her seat after a nursing break. "He and Fenna get on like they're made for each other."

"If Emperor Brynt is in, I will start with five-card draw since the betting is relatively uncomplicated," Dring announced. "Everybody please ante."

"That means you put in ten millicreds, one of the yellow chips," Kelly explained to the Cayl. She swapped places with Brynt and dragged up another of the lightweight carbon fiber chairs to sit at his shoulder.

"Can I put in more?" the emperor asked.

"Why would you want to do that?" Dring inquired.

"As a statement," Brynt replied. "I wouldn't want anybody to confuse my participation in this game with avarice."

"But even with the explanation, you're the only one who would appreciate the gesture," Kelly argued. "It's like the apocryphal story about the man who walked fast on his way to church every Sunday and dragged his feet on the way home. He wanted everybody to see how eager he was to enter the House of the Lord and how reluctant he was to leave, but the only one he ended up impressing was himself."

The Cayl twisted his shaggy head sharply to look at the EarthCent ambassador. "Are you suggesting that the other species are laughing behind our backs?"

"Let me put it this way," Jeeves said. "This is an exclusive poker game. We don't invite just anybody to sit in."

"What the young Stryx is trying to express is that most sentients will gladly entertain the foibles of aliens when there's a profit in doing so," Dring explained as he completed the deal. "It has been a long time since I visited your region of space, but I do seem to recall visiting a market where two prices were displayed for every item on sale."

"Wholesale and retail?" Blythe asked, sorting the cards in her hand.

"Cayl and Native," Dring replied. "It struck me as odd so I asked about it. This particular market was next to a Cayl garrison post, and some of the vendors had discovered they could attract more business by displaying a higher price for the warriors."

"It does sound a bit like an affectation when you put it that way," the emperor mumbled, picking up his own cards and spreading them into a fan shape. "Did you say that three of one kind and two of another kind is a good hand?"

Joe groaned and threw his cards into the center of the table, followed by everybody else in turn, except for Dring.

"It is a very good hand if you're talking about the rank of the card, like matching numbers or pictures," the Maker replied. "If you're talking about the suit, like a red heart or diamond, or a black club or spade, then you'll want to draw new cards. Would you like to place a bet?"

"How many new cards can I ask for?"

"You may discard up to three cards in return for an equal number of replacements. Some people allow four cards to be drawn if you hold an ace, but as the dealer, I don't allow that."

"Then I won't bet," Brynt said.

Shaina banged her head on the table, then laughed and turned to Jeeves. "That's the first time I've seen you bluffed out by table talk," she said to the Stryx.

"I never believed he drew a full house on the deal," Jeeves replied stiffly. "I would have folded these cards no matter what."

"Somebody is full of something," Shaina said in a sotto voice.

"I will also pass," Dring said, setting down his hand and picking up the deck. "How many cards do you want?"

Kelly surveyed the hand the Cayl emperor held up for her, and then tapped a couple of the cards.

"Two," Brynt said, discarding the cards Kelly had selected.

"Those were the ones I wanted you to keep," Kelly blurted. "Oh, forget you heard that, Dring."

"Dealer takes one," Dring said, exchanging a card for himself. "Do you wish to bet now?"

Brynt held his modified hand up for the EarthCent ambassador, who nodded and pointed at the blue stack. The emperor slid the whole pile into the pot.

"I meant one chip!" Kelly exploded. "Don't you guys do anything in moderation?"

Dring looked at Kelly, looked at the Cayl, and then looked back at Kelly again. "I fold," he announced.

"So these win?" the emperor asked in amazement. He laid out his hand, which consisted of a pair of fives and three unmatched face cards.

"You don't have to show them," Kelly said. "You win as soon as everybody else folds."

"But that's fascinating," Brynt declared. "It means I can represent holding better cards than those I've drawn. It's as if I could approach a planet in a shuttle while appearing on their detection grid as a war fleet. What's to prevent me from doing this every hand?"

"In this case, you had me beat," Dring said, flipping over his cards to show a missed straight. "But remember, if you bluff that you are holding better cards every time, eventually somebody who draws a strong hand will

146

challenge you, and then you'll lose the large number of chips you have put in the pot."

"I understand," the emperor said, leaning back in his chair. He fished in his belt pouch for a hard biscuit and bit into it with a loud crunch. Beowulf appeared out of nowhere and dropped his giant head in the Cayl's lap.

"Don't beg, boy," Joe said. "I'll get more pretzels." He rose from the table and took the empty pitcher with him.

"One," Brynt said, giving the dog a biscuit. "They're good for the teeth."

"Even if you don't chew them?" Shaina remarked.

Beowulf ingested the biscuit and did his best to pretend he didn't know what "one" meant. The Cayl pushed the dog away.

"My deal," Clive said, retrieving the deck from the Maker. "I think explaining seven-card stud to Emperor Brynt will give Joe enough time to get back with the goodies."

"Your parents have returned to Earth without you?" Brynt asked the EarthCent ambassador.

"Yes," Kelly said. "I saw them off this morning while Daniel was showing you and the others around Libbyland. Did you think my parents lived here with us all of the time?"

"They were here when I arrived," the Cayl observed. "Many species have such living arrangements. There are times I regret that we have always fostered a tradition of encouraging our young to go out to test their mettle. Many of them never return."

"I've come across several large Cayl colonies in my travels," Dring commented. He peeked at his first hole card as soon as it landed in front of him. "Your people do pick some of the least hospitable places to settle. I remember one world in the Orion Nebula which was completely covered in ice for half of its year and uncomfortably hot and wet for the other half. The colonists constructed cities and farms floating in the atmosphere, with agricultural fields that were irrigated from the bottom by natural steam. The vegetables were delicious."

"Don't you keep in contact with the Cayl who emigrate?" Kelly asked. "Surely your science is capable of it."

"For millions of years we have built our colony ship fleets for one-way trips," Brynt replied. "The vessels are engineered for reuse as components of warships, power plants, laboratories and workshops. Even the floating cities our friend just mentioned are likely based on the colony ship platform. It would be shameful to burden our pioneers with a reporting requirement, as if we didn't trust them to succeed."

"Let me get this straight," Blythe said. "Whenever your people build up enough population and resources to equip an expedition, you sent away a colony fleet and you don't even maintain trade relations?"

"Trade is for the moneylenders," the Cayl replied dismissively. Now that he had two cards before him, he took a peek, and then remembered to hold them up for Kelly. "No offense to any businessmen present."

"None taken," Jeeves responded. "Our archives include regular contacts with a number of successful Cayl colonies, though none of them have developed into empires like the parent civilization."

"Of course not," the emperor said, watching the first round of face-up cards being dealt. "They would have learned from our example the expense and aggravation of maintaining an empire."

"And you aren't even curious to know how they're doing?" Jeeves pursued the question while examining his own cards. "You've never thought of sending a ship just to check in?"

"It could be interpreted the wrong way, as if we didn't trust them," Brynt explained. "How would you like it if your progenitors watched you all of the time?"

"They do," Jeeves muttered.

"But what if your colonists are thinking exactly the same way you are?" Kelly demanded. "What if they're too proud to contact you for fear you'll think they need help?"

"What should I do?" the Cayl asked the ambassador.

"You should reach out to them," Kelly said, warming to her subject. "You're the emperor. You can stand up and change a mistaken tradition that's persisted for millions of years!"

"I meant, what should I do with these cards?"

"Oh. The betting starts to the left of the dealer, so you don't have to do anything yet." Everybody passed until the bet reached the emperor, at which point Kelly said, "I guess I'd raise a yellow. Just one," she admonished, as the Cayl toyed with the stack. "You have three more open cards and another hole card to come."

Dring, Daniel, Shaina and Blythe all folded. Kelly reached over and pushed in a yellow chip for Joe's hand without looking at his hole cards. Clive gave the remaining players a second face-up card, maintaining a running commentary.

"Lady for the emperor, Nine for the Stryx, Joe pairs his Four, and an Ace for the dealer."

"I don't want to sound nosy, but doesn't your intelligence service have any information about the Cayl who have emigrated?" Blythe asked.

149

"We don't have an intelligence service," the emperor responded. He appeared to be distracted as he puzzled over his hand, attempting to project the possibilities three cards into the future.

"Don't tell me," Blythe said. "The Cayl see spying as dishonorable."

"In some cases," the emperor replied. "What if I stationed agents behind each of you to report on your cards?"

"Cheating is different," Blythe protested.

"Is it?" the Cayl asked. "The histories record that the Empire maintained an intelligence service in its early days, but it was abandoned due to ballooning costs. Besides, there are some things that an emperor is better off not knowing about his subjects."

"It's me?" Joe said, returning to the table with a pitcher of beer and the pretzels. After glancing at his hole cards, he announced, "Fours bet a hundred," and pushed a red chip into the center of the table.

Jeeves, the Cayl and Clive all called, and the head of EarthCent Intelligence dealt a third open card. Joe's pair of Fours held up, but Jeeves showed three diamonds that could potentially be connected in a straight flush. Joe poured himself a beer to buy time for thinking.

"Did I tell you that Jonah is quitting dancing?" Blythe asked Kelly. "Vivian was so disappointed, but we explained to her that it's unfair to make her brother continue just so she'll have a partner."

"Can't Marcus find her a boy to dance with? I thought his school was doing very well."

"It is, but almost all of his students are adults. Most kids aren't interested in ballroom dancing. She's probably going to have to give it up."

"Samuel wants to learn ballroom dancing," Jeeves mentioned offhandedly.

"Our Samuel?" Kelly asked in surprise. "What gave you that idea?"

"I hear things. I'll bet you ten creds I'm right."

"Done," Kelly said impulsively.

"Are the suits all equivalent?" the Cayl asked. "If the Stryx and I held the same suited progression of ranks, would his diamonds be worth more than my clubs?"

"We don't use suits in ranking hands," Clive replied, taking another look at the Cayl's exposed cards. "But if you're trying to represent a straight flush, you don't—oh wait, I guess you do have a shot, though you'll need some luck getting there."

"Fours bet a hundred," Joe said again, pushing another red chip into the pot. "Beowulf. Go find Samuel."

"He and Banger were playing in my garden when I left," Dring said. The dog trotted off in the direction of Dring's corner of the hold.

"See your hundred, and I'll raise a thousand," Jeeves declared, pushing a red and a blue into the center of the table with his pincer. The Cayl did the same, but Clive folded. Joe grimaced, but he paid the blue to see another card.

"Fours triple up," Clive announced, as he went around the table dealing the remaining three players their final open card. "Straight flush still possible for Jeeves, outside shot at a straight flush for the Emperor. Fours bet."

"Five thousand," Joe declared without hesitation, pushing five blues into the growing pile.

"Is that a lot?" Brynt asked.

"Well, it's a lot for this game," Kelly replied.

151

"We play for millicreds," Shaina explained. "A blue chip is one cred, enough to buy a cup of coffee in some places."

"Call," Jeeves said, moving five blues into the pot.

"Well, it's your money," the Emperor said to Kelly. "What do you think?"

"Let me see them again." The Cayl held up his hole cards, cupped between his two large hands. Kelly looked at the cards, studied her husband's face for a moment, and decided he looked far too relaxed for her liking. Besides, Jeeves had a better chance of making a flush, if he didn't have one already. "Let's fold," she said.

Clive dealt a final face-down card to Joe and the Stryx.

"Did you get it?" Joe asked the Stryx.

"Are you passing or are you just making conversation?" Jeeves replied.

"I guess there's no point trying to read you," Joe said. "I'll just play the odds." He counted his remaining blue chips and pushed them in. "Bet's twelve thousand."

"Twelve thousand sounds so much cooler than twelve creds," Shaina pointed out for the Cayl's benefit.

"Every human has his day," Jeeves muttered, conceding the hand.

Joe raked in the chips and began building stacks as Clive passed the remains of the deck to Blythe.

"Back to five-card draw," she announced, accepting the scattered discards and straightening out the deck for shuffling. "I'll bet this is the first time in history that a human beat out a Cayl, a Stryx and a Maker for a pot."

"That's right," Kelly said. "You made history, Joe."

"Doesn't count," Joe replied complacently. "It would be like Beowulf taking credit for being the first dog to eat a Cayl biscuit and a handful of pretzels with a Stryx and a Maker present at the same time. It's got everything to do with the guest list and nothing to do with the accomplishment."

Samuel reached the table at a run, Banger floating beside him and Beowulf nipping at his heels. "What is it?" he panted.

"Jonah doesn't want to take dance lessons with his sister anymore," Joe addressed his son. "Jeeves said you might be interested."

"Okay," the boy said. "When do I start?"

"Okay?" Kelly pulled her son over and looked him in the eye. "Since when are you interested in dancing?"

"I always liked dancing," Samuel said evasively. "Don't you remember when I used to practice with Aisha?"

"But you were always making fun of her," Kelly reminded him.

"When do I start?" Samuel repeated, going around to where Blythe sat and attempting to look angelic. He came across more like a hungry dog, which made perfect sense, since his acting coach was Beowulf.

"They've been practicing every afternoon for three hours after they get out of Libby's school," Blythe said. "I'll talk to Marcus about reducing the time."

"Three hours is good," Samuel insisted. "I'll learn faster that way. Can Banger come?"

"I don't see why not," Blythe replied. "Well, this will make Vivian a happy little girl, but let's tell her that's it's just an experiment, Samuel. I wouldn't want to disappoint her if you don't like it."

"I'll like it," Samuel said confidently.

As soon as the boy headed into the ice harvester with the little Stryx to get ready for bed, Jeeves gave a fair imitation of a throat-clearing sound.

153

"Joe?" Kelly asked. "Think you could slide Jeeves ten blues for me since you're doing so well? I don't want to put Emperor Brynt on a short stack."

Fourteen

"Watch your step," Pava told the hostages apologetically as she led them into the imperial dining room. "The deck is a little irregular because some of the airtight bulkheads below collapsed when the palace crash-landed."

Lynx stumbled as a cub bounced off her ankles, the fifth in line to be the next emperor, if she recalled. The Cayl females were much smaller than the males, and the cubs looked like little white balls of fur. Amazingly, the eyes of the young Cayl remained shut until well after they were weaned, but that didn't stop them from racing around the palace at breakneck speed, relying on imperfectly developed echo sounding.

"It's a beautiful room," Brinda said. "I haven't seen so much wonderful art in one place since the Kasilian auction."

"Gifts, mainly," the empress said, guiding them to seats at the well-appointed table. "Please pick something out to take home with you. I don't know what I'm going to do with it all if we have to move."

"Is the orange tape on the table for us?" Lynx asked.

"To protect you," Pava replied. "I'm afraid that the biological scans I did of your cell structure and my analysis of your microbiota indicate that your bodies are unable to tolerate any of our natural foodstuffs. I've invited the ambassadors of the four leading species of the empire in

155

your honor. They're such wonderfully pushy people that I'm afraid they might talk you into trying some local delicacy unless I put a clear boundary in place."

"You all eat the same food?" Woojin asked.

"I only serve dishes that everybody can enjoy together at official meals," the empress explained. "Every species has adaptations to certain foodstuffs that are unlikely to be replicated in the others, but after millions of years of trade in the empire, there's a great deal of common cuisine available."

A raucous barking from the pack of hounds that ran freely through the palace penetrated to the dining room.

"Oh, I expect that's my guests now," Pava continued. "Remember, they're very sensitive souls and easily cowed, so please don't comment on their funny looks. The poor Lood even wears a mask so that the other aliens don't stare at his third eye."

"Do you meet with the aliens often?" Lynx asked. "Just my professional curiosity, as a cultural attaché."

"Believe it or not, my husband doesn't care for them," Pava admitted. "He says that I only see them on their best behavior, and that away from our influence, they are shockingly rude. But I find them quite amusing, and I choose to judge others by their actions and not their reputations."

Four aliens swept into the room, accompanied by Gurf and a half a dozen of the larger hounds. After the empress made introductions all the way around and the aliens took their seats, the dogs sat down behind them.

"Isn't it cute?" Pava whispered to Lynx. "The hounds worry about me being alone with the ambassadors while Brynt is away, so they've appointed themselves as my guards."

"I'm disappointed to hear that you'll be unable to partake in our common dishes," the Lood ambassador addressed the humans in a hearty tone. "I assure you that Empress Pava is a wonderful cook, and her interpretation of Cuy stew is the best I've ever tasted."

"You've stolen the words from my mouth, Z'tan," the Nangor ambassador protested. "Here, let me fill everybody's glass for a toast. No, don't stand, Empress. I'll go around the table."

"Just halfway please," the Tzvim ambassador said, as the Nangor neatly poured a glowing pink fluid into her glass. "Thank you, Rimad."

"You're most welcome, Keef," the Nangor responded politely, before moving on to the Shuga. "Your usual measure, Arnbal?"

"Yes, thank you, Rimad," the bird-like alien practically purred.

Woojin took up the decanter of synthesized human wine and filled the glasses of his companions without rising from his seat. Lynx took the opportunity to whisper in his ear, "If this is how the aliens of the Cayl Empire always conduct themselves, the tunnel network species are going to eat them alive."

"Empress?" the Nangor asked, pausing before he approached her. "May I do the honors?"

"Of course, Rimad," Pava said, pushing her guardian hound's head out of the way.

The Nangor leaned forward cautiously, keeping one eye on Gurf, and was careful not to make any sudden moves with his trunk as he filled Pava's glass. "Will the Dowager Empress be joining us?"

"Not this evening," the empress said. "She's trying to repair our old tachyon fountain so the younger cubs can get a chance to play with it. When I last saw her, she was up to her elbows in probability detectors that were almost as old as the palace."

"As is she," Z'tan said in a stage whisper, bringing a round of chuckles from the other ambassadors and an involuntary grin from the daughter-in-law of the Dowager Empress. "But seriously," the Lood continued, adjusting his gold mask up a little so that the mouth opening was better aligned with his lips. "It's always been a wonder to me how the two of you keep this place functioning without any staff."

"Hear, hear," the Nangor said, lifting his glass high. "A toast to the First Ladies of the Empire, may their experiments forever prove their theories."

The three humans hoisted their glasses dutifully and drank along with the five aliens. Whatever method the Cayl had used for synthesizing the wine, it was the best any of them had ever tasted, and Brinda hastened to compliment the empress.

"Oh, no," Pava protested. "I got the recipe from your Stryx friends before you arrived. And, Rimad," she continued, turning to the Nangor. "You know perfectly well that experiments which disprove theories are just as valuable as those which confirm them. It would be a boring universe indeed if we got everything right the first time."

A medium-size Cayl came cannoning into the dining room and scrabbled to a halt next to Pava's chair.

"Grams, come quick. Bodu ate something he caught in the garden and now he's throwing up all over the place!"

"Excuse me," Pava said, leaping from her chair and dropping to all fours. "Please make yourselves at home until I return." Then she sprinted off, her granddaughter in hot pursuit. Several of the hounds charged after them, but

Gurf and three of the larger males maintained their vigil over the ambassadors.

"I hope the poor little cub is alright," Brinda said. "It's no fun being sick when you're young."

"Happens at least once every state dinner," the Tzvim ambassador replied dismissively. "Cayl young eat everything they find on the ground, just like their dogs."

Gurf growled a warning.

"Look, she could be back any time, so let's get down to business," the Lood ambassador said. "The four of us didn't accept posting to this miserable planet for our health. Business at my embassy pawn shop is off ninety percent since that fool of an emperor announced he was dissolving the empire. The short-term contract the Cayl negotiated for extending their protection has resulted in the host worlds actually covering garrison expenses for the first time. That means the families of the warriors have stopped pawning their heirlooms to send money to their sons and dogs to keep them fed."

"And as business rolls downhill, volume at my money transfer agency has collapsed," the Shuga said angrily. "Without the three-percent fee and a little fun with the exchange rates, I'm stuck running my embassy at a loss."

"If you think you're in trouble, how about our allowance funds?" the Nangor demanded. "We had most of the Cayl in the capital giving us their cash in return for an allowance so they wouldn't have to dirty themselves with holding money. Now, for the first time ever they're all asking for the money at the same time, in case they have to move. How are we supposed to meet their demands?"

"It's tied up in long-term investments?" Lynx asked.

The four ambassadors looked at the human, then broke out laughing. The Nangor wheezed like he had something stuck in his trunk.

The Tzvim recovered first and informed the humans, "The Nangors spend the money as it comes in. The Cayl are idiots. All that matters to them is science and fighting. Do you see that Shiduck hanging over there?"

The humans turned in the direction the Tzvim was pointing, but the wall was so covered with art they couldn't tell which piece the alien ambassador was talking about.

"The big green square with the dot of white in the middle. I traded it to the empress for a Phwealleet that was presented to the imperial family at the Treaty of Sh'dad. I made a thousand percent on the deal."

"A male would have given it to you as a gift," the Shuga said. "The females are the ones who handle the household finances and they aren't entirely stupid. I've never been able to get one to borrow money on any terms."

"You don't worry that the Cayl might be listening in while you tell us this?" Woojin asked, taken aback by the audacity of the ambassadors.

"Wouldn't be honorable," the Lood replied in a mocking tone. "Violating the privacy of guests and all that nonsense. My fellow ambassadors and I aren't greedy people, but neither are we fools. You just stay out of our business and we'll stay out of yours."

"It won't be hard for you to stay out of our business because we don't have any," Lynx told the ambassador bluntly. "We thought we were coming just to have a look around, but it turns out that we're hostages for the safe return of the emperor. We don't know much about how this empire works, but it looks to me like you're doing your best to bite the hand that feeds you."

"Would you excuse us for a moment?" the Lood said. The three other ambassadors looked at him questioningly, but they followed when he rose from his seat and led them over to a statue of a creature that looked like a giant crab.

"I don't like the way the Lood reacted when you told him we're hostages for the safe return of the emperor," Woojin said softly. "It's pretty clear that the ambassadors aren't happy with the new state of affairs."

"You mean they might think that by, uh, eliminating us, they could keep the emperor from returning?" Brinda asked.

"That's how hostage exchanges normally work," Woojin said. "If they come back with suggestions for sightseeing or invitations to visit their embassies, I suggest we plead scheduling conflicts."

The empress returned to the dining hall, the fur on her stomach looking a bit damp, as if she had just washed something out of it. The ambassadors hurried back to their seats, and with the exception of the Lood, whose features were hidden, they all looked rather pleased with themselves.

"Oh, you waited for me to start," Pava said, looking at the untouched serving dishes. "I'm honored by your regard, but it's a shame to let food go cold."

"I'd rather eat cold Cuy stew made by your hands than the pale imitation available elsewhere," the Lood declared gallantly. "May I propose another toast?"

"As you wish," Pava said shyly.

"To the safe return of Emperor Brynt!"

"Hear, hear," the three ambassadors chimed in, blatantly eyeing the humans.

161

"Thank you, my friends," the empress replied. "Now let's eat while it's still lukewarm."

It quickly became apparent to the hostages that the scheming ambassadors hadn't been play-acting when praising Pava's cooking. Even though the human-compatible dishes were all cooked from synthesized ingredients which the Cayl had never seen before, the food tasted as good as the wine. Lynx recognized the lamb stew as something Ian's wife was fond of making, so she assumed that Jeeves had passed along the recipes.

"Everything was absolutely delicious," Z'tan declared when the serving dishes were empty. He delicately wiped a bit of gravy from the chin of his golden mask.

"It's such a shame that the young cub got sick," Rimad said in a heartfelt tone. "Don't you think you could change the rules just once?" he added slyly.

Gurf growled again.

"I'm afraid there you have it, gentlemen," the empress said sadly. "State dinners are limited to a single evening division, and it appears our time is almost up."

"I would like to extend the hospitality of the Tzvim embassy to your guests," Keef said. "Perhaps I could escort them on a daytrip to the Cliff of Heroes."

"Yes, my embassy would be honored as well," the Shuga said. "You know I would never miss an opportunity to build intercultural understanding. The Humans might enjoy a visit to the Poison Woods, wearing our protective clothing, of course."

"Have you ever been boating in white water?" Rimad asked the hostages. "There's a stretch of river not far from here that's unmatched in the empire for a thrilling ride."

"I was planning on an outing to Death Gorge in the near future myself," Z'tan said. "It would be no trouble at all to bring three guests along."

"No, no," the empress said, holding up her hands to restrain the would-be tour guides. "I'm afraid the protocol for hostages is that I must keep them on the palace grounds. However, if they choose to remain for a vacation on Cayl after the emperor returns, I'm sure they will consider your hospitality."

The Tzvim began to protest, but the large Cayl hound behind his seat lazily scratched the ambassador's turtle-like shell, making a loud sound. The four aliens quickly rose to their feet.

"Thank you so much for having us, Empress," the Lood spoke for them all. "If you reconsider, we'd be more than happy to watch your hostages for you."

"Time, gentlemen," Pava reminded them, showing her fangs in a cheerful smile. "We must abide by the rules."

The ambassadors trooped out of the dining room with the dogs at their heels. The empress relaxed in her chair, looking at the humans expectantly.

"I wasn't going to say anything, but those ambassadors weren't very nice," Lynx blurted out.

"No, I don't expect they were," the Cayl said, a twinkle in her black eyes. "But as I mentioned earlier, I think it's better that we all get a chance to form our own impressions of people."

"They seem pretty intent on cheating you," Brinda ventured. "Stryx Vrine explained in our briefing that the Cayl avoid accumulating excess wealth and treat money as a necessary evil. But I'm a professional auctioneer, and I hate to hear of somebody trading in art so far below the market value."

"Are you referring to my Shiduck?" The empress pointed at the work of art.

"He said the Phweealleet you swapped for it was worth ten times as much."

"It would have been, if it was an original," Pava replied with a chuckle. "Of course, my husband's family is chronically in need of funds, and the real painting was sold before the blood was dry on the treaty."

Brinda snorted, and a smile spread over her face. "How about the pawn shop for heirlooms run by Z'tan?"

"It's funny how the species of our own empire treat us like fools," the empress replied. "We have such a reputation for honesty that nobody ever bothers to ask why we never run out of heirlooms. I've sold the Lood a number of primitive ceramics made by the cubs at a very good price. I suspect he believes they are antiques from one of our arts-and-crafts movements that come along every million years or so but he's never inquired, likely for fear of tipping me off to the assumed value."

"Your grandchildren just happen to throw pottery that looks like something from your history?" Lynx asked.

"I may have given them a few holograms to look at, and Brynt's mother helps with the glaze," the empress said playfully.

"How about the allowance fund the Nangor was talking about?" Woojin asked. "That sounded like the sort of thing that caused Earth's economy to collapse."

"It's how the Cayl in the capital currently get rid of excess income, which is not a problem we ever have around the palace," the empress said ruefully. "Many of our people take a break from basic research now and then to dabble in freelance technology work for the various species of our empire. Some of the solutions result in patents or

164

licensing agreements that create more income than can be spent on new lab equipment and other essentials. Those Cayl divide the leftover between the colony fleet fund and playing along with the schemes of whatever species needs some financial propping up."

"You know, that's sort of the same way the Stryx run things," Brinda said. "They don't put garrisons on planets, but the main thing keeping the tunnel network together is economic incentives. You do the same thing in a different way."

"We would never think to compare ourselves with your Stryx," the empress said modestly. "One of our greatest scientists proved a thousand generations ago that it's impossible to solve the basic multiverse equations without scalable artificial intelligence. Still, we chip away at the dimensional membrane using an experimental approach, and the Stryx promise to let us know if we put the universe in danger."

Fifteen

"I thought you'd never done this before and I was going to be your teacher," Dorothy said in a disappointed tone. "I've been coming here since before it was open, but you're obviously better at flying than me. I only asked Paul to let us in early and turn on this little practice area because I was worried you'd get airsick."

"I spent weeks at a time in near Zero-G," David explained. "The miners would set up an atmosphere retention field around an asteroid and bring in bottled air and recycling equipment, just like it was a ship. As long as you used a safety tether on the surface, it wasn't that dangerous. Sometimes they netted off whole sections to cut down on drift accidents."

"Drift accidents?" Dorothy asked.

"The atmosphere retention field only held in gasses. A human body drifts right through it, and then you're in the vacuum. I've seen it happen when kids got careless."

"Kids?"

"All of the mining outfits use kids as powder monkeys. It takes a long time and a lot of energy for a laser to drill a pilot tunnel in rock, so they use skinny kids to set the charges. You go in the pilot hole with a rope around your ankles so they can pull you out, and then everybody stands clear and you hope that the whole asteroid doesn't fall apart when the charge blows. The goal is to break up a lot of rock and collapse the tunnel without too much ejection. After that, it's easy digging to extract and process the rubble."

"How old were you when you starting doing this?" Dorothy asked, as the two teenagers unconsciously synchronized flying movements. Their baskets dangled by short lanyards from their wrists, and they had their faceshields raised for conversation.

"I don't know. Pretty young, I guess," David replied, in sudden embarrassment. "When does the shooting start? I'll bet I don't even get hit. I've had lots of practice dodging rocks."

"They're just paintballs. Paul said the targeting is all automated now, but Jeeves still likes coming in and running it manually. Think of us as the ducks in a Stryx shooting gallery."

"Is your dog going to keep walking around below us all night?" David asked.

Now it was Dorothy's turn to be embarrassed. "My mom said it was my dad's idea for him to come along, and my dad said that Beowulf makes up his own mind about where he goes. Anyway, I can tell from the way he looks at you all the time that he likes you."

"He looks at me like I'm food."

The calliope music began to blare, and a mob rushed into the demarcated levitation area from the rentals lobby. Some of them were frequent players who had already bought levitation suits rather than renting every time they came, and most of them had at least partially donned the gear while waiting for the ride to open.

"It's going to get crowded soon," Dorothy said unnecessarily, maneuvering alongside David and speaking twice as loud as earlier to be heard over the steam organ. "I've

167

never seen so many aliens in the crowd. They must be open house guests from the Cayl Empire."

"Aliens all look pretty much the same to me," David replied. "I can tell the four-armed ones apart from everybody else, and the ones with vines for hair, they're Drazens, right?"

"Frunge," Dorothy said, taking David's arm and pulling him closer so they could hear each other without shouting. She heard Beowulf bark to inform her they were close enough. "Until you make some alien friends, it's probably hard to keep the names of their species straight. See the tall guy with four arms pulling on the orange suit? He's a Dollnick, but the one over there with four arms and an elephant head? He's one of the new aliens from the Cayl Empire."

"Do you have any idea why the Stryx want all of these new species to join the tunnel network? Don't they have enough aliens already?"

"It's complicated," Dorothy replied, falling back on one of her favorite expressions. "The Stryx don't like to see biologicals or any other sentients going to war with each other. So they offer benefits to the species that join up with the tunnel network in return for not fighting interplanetary wars, though they can do what they want at home. The Cayl Empire is sort of the same, but different. Well, the results are sort of the same. They mainly live in peace and trade a lot with each other, and the Cayl keep everybody in line. But with the Cayl getting out of the empire business, I guess the Stryx think somebody else needs to take over and keep things peaceful."

"Sounds like a lot of work," David commented. "What's the guy with the grey feathers there?"

"It's a she, a Fillinduck. The one over there with all the red and blue feathers is a male Fillinduck, and the silvery one with the feathers on his head giving Paul a hard time is one of the new aliens."

"I think he's mad that the helmet won't fit over his crest," David said, watching the irate Shuga pantomiming his complaint. "This is almost like being in school."

"What 'this'? Our date?"

The gangly boy mumbled something about wanting to try the Physics Ride and not wanting to come alone.

"You came to the lost-and-found and asked me out, so it's a date, my first one," Dorothy informed him. "If you don't believe me, ask Beowulf." Then she relented since he looked so embarrassed that she was afraid he'd fly away. "So did you get to go to school when you were working as a miner?"

"No, but there were always teacher bots around to learn stuff from when we weren't working. I guess the Stryx practically give them away, so the miners saw it as cheap entertainment to keep the kids out of trouble. And they used to rotate us between planetary mining and asteroids, because if you stay in Zero-G too long, your bones don't grow right and you get too weak to work. Sometimes on a planet we'd have a visiting teacher for a while, if they could find one who was cheap enough."

"So they let you off the asteroids to get healthy so you could work more, just like you were mining ponies," Dorothy said, her eyes tearing up. "Sometime I wish the Stryx would just take everything over and make people be good to each other, but Libby says that no sentients really want somebody telling them how to live."

"Who's the guy with the golden mask?" David asked, mainly to change the subject.

"Another one of the new aliens. Their ruling class supposedly have a third eye behind the mask, and they can make some people do stuff, like the high-caste Vergallian women."

"The Vergallians are the ones who look like humans?"

"The ones from the ruling classes are all beautiful, like actors in immersives, only more perfect. The women produce a mix of pheromones that can make men crazy, so just stay away from them," she warned him.

The main levitation chamber of the Physics Ride began to power up, and thousands of players swam upwards through the air. Some began to experiment with acrobatic moves as soon as their feet left the ground, others concentrated on just controlling which way they were facing.

"Is everybody ready for the Physics Ride?" Jeeves boomed over the helmet speakers. The floating mass of players cheered in response.

"Get your basket ready," Dorothy urged her date. "Not getting hit is good, but catching and shooting back is how you score points. They put up a scrolling leaderboard last week, so if you get into the top fifty, you'll see your name and score go by."

"First round, target-practice," Jeeves declared. "Five points for a basket. Ten points for a hit."

"Hit what?" David asked his date. "Are we supposed to shoot at each other?"

"There are discs floating around the edge of the flying space—there's one now," Dorothy said, pointing at a paint-spattered object. "My little brother is really good at hitting them, but I usually miss unless I'm moving in the same direction at about the same speed."

"But we don't get any ammunition to shoot unless we catch it?"

"I'm good at catching. I can give you the paintballs I catch if you can't snag any."

"I'll have to see how fast everything moves," David replied. "We used to throw rocks in the air and then try to hit them with other rocks, so I'm pretty good at timing. There's not much else to do on an asteroid," he added by way of explanation.

The first colored balls began whizzing towards the crowd, and thanks to their position at the far edge, Dorothy and David were able to see them coming from a distance. Both had a catch within the first few seconds, and David pinged his off a floating disc like he'd been playing all his life. Dorothy's return shot sailed wide.

"You almost got it," the boy said encouragingly.

"Did not," Dorothy replied. "It's all right. Nobody is good at everything, except maybe Blythe and Chastity, but they don't count."

"What happens if we get hit?"

"The suit keeps track and reports back to the levitation controller. If you get hit three times, you're declared a casualty and you drop out of the action."

"What if you don't want to quit?"

"It's not up to you," Dorothy explained. "The suit just stops responding to what you do and puts you down. Paul says that all of the computations involved to keep thousands of people flying around in here at the same time would tax a planetary-defense system, but Jeeves repurposed a Verlock weather simulator to do the math."

"Oh," David replied, not knowing what else to say. "Watch it!" He stuck his basket out behind her to catch a paintball he'd seen out of the corner of his eye coming at them through the crowd. Then he turned and splashed it off one of the moving targets without seeming to try.

171

"Maybe we should fly back-to-back so we can see the stuff that makes it through the crowd."

"But how will we know if we start floating apart?"

"You watch the outside and I'll watch the inside and make sure we keep close," the boy replied. "The other powder monkeys always said that I had eyes in the back of my head."

The pair made it through the first round without getting hit, and David racked up enough points with his uncanny accuracy on the returns for his name to appear on the leaderboard. Just as the clock was winding down on the first round, the music from the steam organ rose to a cacophonous wail, and Dorothy saw Paul running towards it. Then the noise gave way to an eerie silence.

"The roll must have ripped," Dorothy commented to David, her voice sounding unnaturally loud in her own ears.

"I was just getting used to it. Without the music, it kind of feels like being back on an asteroid. I'll probably have a bad dream tonight about my tether breaking."

"Praise Hwarith that horrendous noise has stopped," a nearby flier remarked loudly to his companions. "Between the smell of these Union Station species and the noise they pass off as music, I'm ready to go home."

"Did you see the old Human working on that silly contraption while we were here yesterday?" asked another of the golden-masked fliers. "A natural slave race, if I've ever seen one."

"You take that back," Dorothy exclaimed, turning on the trio of Loods. Two of them wore the golden mask of the ruling class, and the third might have been a family servant. "My father imported that steam organ from Earth and it's a genuine antique. That's what they're supposed to sound like."

"What have we here?" the first Lood speaker said, turning towards Dorothy. "The face isn't bad. Is it for sale? Ask it if it has a price," he added, addressing the third member of the trio.

"My Lord Z'fark wishes to know your price," the factotum relayed politely.

Dorothy turned bright red and clenched her fists, the first time in her young life she found herself at a loss for words.

"What are they saying?" David demanded. He suddenly regretted not accepting Ian's offer to advance him the cost of a translation implant. Dorothy had told him it was best to get a high-quality one with subvoc capability, so he was saving his money.

"Second round," Jeeves announced over their helmet speakers. "Elimination. Get ten points for every player you shoot, lose fifteen if you get hit. If your point total goes negative, you're out."

"They were making fun of the steam organ my father rebuilt," Dorothy told David, unwilling to reproduce the actual conversation. "The two with the masks are some kind of higher-ups who are too good to speak to humans."

A blue ball came whizzing in from the perimeter, and David caught it effortlessly. Then he turned and pressed the button on the handle, shooting one of the gold-masked Loods in the chest at point-blank range.

"Get him," the enraged young Lood shouted at the servant.

The third alien groped at his ankle for a boot knife, but the wrap-around levitation suit covered the handle. So he kicked his legs and tried to fly at David, but the latter

easily avoided the attack. While the servant was awkwardly executing a turn, he was hit by a green paintball fired by
another member of the crowd and lost control, the levitation suit returning him to the deck.

"He didn't have any points saved up so the first hit took
him out," Dorothy exclaimed. "Look, his friends didn't
even let him have a basket."

The two gold-masked Loods remained floating a short
distance away, barking orders at each other.

"Let's take them down."

"You expect me to touch those things?"

"Then catch some balls and shoot them."

"Why don't we hang gold and make them shoot each
other?"

As they argued, David caught another ball and shot the
second Lood in the chest.

"No!" the boy's first victim remonstrated, reaching over
and preventing his companion from removing his mask.
"My father said nobody unmasks without permission.
Besides, you wouldn't want to lose your third eye to a stray
ball."

Dorothy caught a ball and splattered it right over the
one David had recently delivered. She was pleased to
discover that shooting floating humanoids a short distance
away was much easier than hitting disc targets moving
rapidly around the perimeter, especially after what the
Lood had said to her.

"Catch balls," ordered the Lood who had been about to
remove his mask, and the two of them began to display
reasonable flying skills, twisting around and watching for
incoming ammunition. As the bulk of the fliers engaged in
a free-for-all, the four enraged combatants at the edge of
the melee concentrated strictly on shooting each other.

174

Dorothy and David targeted each of the Loods equally, but the two aliens focused on getting the boy out of the fight. Fortunately, he had stored up enough points in the first round to hold out, and before the time expired for the second round, the humans had succeeded in eliminating one of the Loods.

"Looks like somebody bit off more than he can chew," Dorothy taunted the remaining Lood, her blood up.

The alien fought to control himself, his hand jerking towards his mask and then away again. Finally, he couldn't restrain himself any longer and spoke directly to Dorothy.

"Easy to talk big in a public space," he snarled. "I'm going to be looking for you."

"You won't have to look," the girl shot back. "My name is Dorothy McAllister and I work at the lost-and-found. Just ask a lift tube."

"Consider it a date," the Lood replied, his tone conveying that he meant it as a threat. As Jeeves announced the third round, Z'fark executed a lazy barrel roll and moved away from the young couple, who clearly had him outgunned.

"What did he say?" David demanded, gripping Dorothy's wrist. "Why did you tell him where to find you? What if he shows up with his friends and I'm not around."

"We're on Union Station," Dorothy said, though she was already beginning to regret her rash statement. "The Stryx are always watching."

"But you said the aliens with the gold masks can make people do stuff," David retorted. "What if he makes you want to leave with him? How are the Stryx supposed to know the difference?"

"Libby would know," Dorothy replied confidently.

Sixteen

Kelly opened the meeting as soon as the Chert un-cloaked. "Thank you all for coming on such short notice. Ambassador Aluria was kind enough to make her conference room available for this emergency consultation, and I want to take a moment to say that the renovations turned out quite nicely."

When the new Vergallian ambassador had arrived on Union Station, she made a point of snubbing the species she didn't approve of by not inviting them to her first official reception. It had backfired when several powerful diplomats turned down her invitation. Now that Aluria found herself needing the EarthCent ambassador's support, being reminded of her earlier mistake was galling, and she was surprised that the human was capable of that degree of subtlety.

"It's a shame I can't say the same about the embassy's wine cellar," Czeros commented, shaking his head over the vintage of Vergallian Yellow on the table. "What's the point of building an empire if you can't make decent wine? In any case, I assume that the true purpose of this meeting is to hear your complaints about the open house guests."

"They're the worst sentients I've ever met," Aluria declared, not even bothering to contradict the Frunge. "The Lood emissary staying in my home is bad enough, but his people are absolute animals. Some of our women have

176

been forced to draw knives to preserve their honor, in public cafés no less!"

"I know that the Stryx have already banned a number of the guests for the duration," Czeros replied, sounding a bit more sympathetic. "We've seen both Loods and Nangors being escorted off of Union Station by bots. One of our merchants from the market deck informed me that the other species are having trouble with a sudden rash of shoplifting, but none of the guests have proven dumb enough to try stealing from a Frunge blade-seller."

"I've heard similar stories from our own merchants, but I wouldn't characterize it as a crime spree quite yet," Kelly said. As the official hostess of the open house, she felt a responsibility not to condemn the guests on anecdotal evidence. "I think it could be a cultural misunderstanding, like if you took your kids somewhere and they acted like they do at home."

"Your children steal from merchants and accost women at home?" Aluria inquired icily.

Kelly decided not to dignify the question with a response.

"I originally took in the alien emissary because I wanted to convince him not to join the tunnel network," Crute admitted, bowing his head as if he were in a Dollnick confessional. "There's plenty of competition around here already, and we've had enough dealings with the Nangors in the past to understand their intentions. But I swear that if those four-armed imposters move to Union Station, I'll resign my post and take my family to live on an all-Dollnick world."

"What have they done?" Kelly asked.

"What haven't they done?" Crute replied in disgust. "My wives are at me constantly not to let Timba near them with that filthy trunk of his. And he expected me to put up his family when they arrived, including his second and third cousins. I told him that if I see another Nangor on our deck, I'm going to have it shredded for fertilizer and sell it to the Frunge."

"I hate to pile on, but I regret inviting the Nangor emissary for dinner," Bork said. "He spent the whole meal cracking tentacle jokes, as if an overgrown nose makes him an expert. I doubt he could even hang from that trunk without breaking his own neck."

"I'd pay to see it," Crute muttered.

"Geed seems very nice," Kelly interjected, hoping to salvage the situation. "I haven't heard any complaints from Grenouthian quarters."

"Then hear them now," the Grenouthian ambassador stated flatly. "The Tzvim is spying on us."

"Maybe she's just very curious about everything," Kelly suggested.

"Our studio engineers were able to crack her in-eye recorder encryption. It turns out she's been copying everything she could get her hands on, including a highly confidential report about the rates for commercial time on our networks which I accidentally left in the bathroom. I should have known something was wrong when she was in there so long, but I assumed she was having trouble using the facilities with that turtle shell of hers."

"What were your engineers doing trying to break into her head?" Kelly asked. The other ambassadors favored her with looks ranging from incredulous to pitying. "Never mind. How about your guest, Ambassador Ortha?"

"Guest?" Ortha said. "Albatross is more like it, if there's a comparable term in your meager language. From the moment that feathered maniac set foot in my home, I haven't had a moment's peace. My children have started taking off their clothes and changing their skin colors to blend in with the furniture when Tarngol is present. I would have sat on my little daughter the other day if she hadn't screamed at the last second."

"Happens in my house all the time," the Chert ambassador commented.

"We are asking the wrong question," the Verlock ambassador rumbled. "Knowing what's at stake, why would they behave so badly?"

"Are you suggesting that they don't want to join the tunnel network anymore than we want them to?" Aluria was obviously taken aback by Srythlan's hypothesis, and her beautiful face did nothing to hide the calculations taking place behind the perfect skin. "It makes sense, unless it's a feint, and they just want us to think they don't want to join so that we won't work to stop them."

"Before somebody takes that logic to the next level of what they think that we think that they think, let me summarize the possibilities," Czeros said. "Either they are acting the way they do because that's how they always act, or they're acting unnaturally because they're trying to pull the vines over our eyes. It's also possible that the Cayl Empire emissaries and their people are reading from different scripts."

"How is it living with the Cayl?" the Chert ambassador inquired.

"Brynt has been the perfect houseguest," Kelly practically gushed. "He eats our food without any problems, he's patient with my nine-year-old boy, and he even plays with the dog. My stepson, Paul, who is a champion Nova player, said that as soon as the Cayl learned the rules, he played like a grandmaster. And when I left home for this

179

meeting, Brynt was helping my husband rebuild a Sharf engine for a small trader."

"Maybe you can get the emperor interested in visiting the hotel district and training the open house guests how to behave," Crute replied sourly.

"He doesn't show any hesitation about disciplining the emissaries when we're together, but Brynt would never do anything that he thought could be interpreted as a criticism of Gryph's management of the station. I recently learned that the Cayl Empire has been sending out colonizing expeditions for millions of years, but they don't keep in touch because they think it could be taken to imply that they doubt the abilities of their emigrants. Their code of honor has evolved to the point that their behavior is frequently irrational and perhaps even self-destructive."

"For a species that knows so little of honor, that's an astute observation," Aluria said grudgingly. "I requested a write-up on the Cayl from the Vergallian Military College, as their academics are the only people I could think of who are interested in species with which we have so little contact. They sent me a one-word answer."

"Are you waiting for a drum-roll?" Bork asked, stealing the thunder from her dramatic pause.

"Selfless," Aluria pronounced, looking rather glum.

"We didn't need to hear that," the Dollnick ambassador said.

"Such was also our assessment," the Grenouthian ambassador concurred.

"Back to the drawing board," Ortha grumbled.

"What's wrong with being selfless?" Kelly asked. "I mean, I wouldn't want my children becoming martyrs, but for the military government of an empire, they could do a lot worse."

"A selfless man is not for sale," the Verlock explained succinctly.

"But the Cayl aren't the ones looking to join the tunnel network," Kelly said. "Oh, wait. Were some of you planning on pooling your resources and bribing the Cayl to keep their empire together?"

"If you had a Shuga sleeping in your home, you'd be thinking the same thing," Ortha said heatedly. "If we thought we could bribe the Stryx not to accept them, we could have kept our business local, but now it's going to come down to what those insufferable emissaries decide to do."

"Why not buy them off?" Kelly inquired sarcastically. "Nobody could accuse the emissaries of being selfless."

"We don't even know if they want to join yet," the Grenouthian ambassador pointed out. "If we show what's in our pouches too early, their price will go up."

"And none of you care that the Stryx believe that getting these species signed up is the right thing to do?"

"Who knows what the Stryx believe," Aluria said dismissively. "If you'd been around as long as the rest of us, you'd have more sense than to take them at their word. If the Stryx really want those species on the tunnel network, they'll get them no matter what anybody does."

"I still think it could all be a giant misunderstanding," Kelly said. "Maybe I'm the only one who sees this because I've been taking the emperor and the four emissaries on outings every day, but the Cayl treats them like overgrown children. He's quick to let them know when they get out of line, but he's just as quick to forgive them."

"So the EarthCent ambassador knows more about the emissaries than those of us who have been hosting them in our homes," Aluria said, a cold smile playing across her face. "I was just thinking that we should approach the emissaries and ask them directly what their intentions are, but I don't feel myself on good enough terms with the Lood to undertake the task.

"I don't have a clue what the Nangor is thinking, if it thinks at all," Crute grunted.

"The Shuga's intentions are impenetrable to me," Ortha added.

"It does seem silly not to employ the services of an expert on the psychology of Cayl Empire species when we have one available," the Grenouthian ambassador added sarcastically.

Kelly groaned inwardly and wondered why she ever opened her mouth in emergency sessions.

"I fail to see the point of sending the EarthCent ambassador to ask the emissaries about their plans," Bork said, coming to the rescue. "Should she also ask them if they're telling the truth? Based on my brief experience with the Nangor, I can see how hosting these alleged diplomats in your homes can be stressful, and clearly it's not giving you the strategic advantage you had counted on. Now that the official open house is underway and the station is flooded with guests, why not tell your temporary lodgers that their presence is needed in the hotels to calm the situation?"

"You mean kick them out?" Ortha mused. "I'm willing."

"Does anybody mind if I consult with the Stryx for a moment?" Kelly asked. She decided to take the look of disgust from Aluria as a sign of acquiescence and spoke out loud. "Libby?"

"Yes, Ambassador," the Stryx librarian responded.

"Now that the official open house is underway, the ambassadors were wondering if it's necessary to continue hosting the emissaries in their homes."

"Union Station is not a penal institution," Libby replied. "If the ambassadors who volunteered to take the emissaries into their homes have run out of patience, I will inform those guests that we are moving them into hotels."

"Without prejudice, Stryx?" the Grenouthian asked.

"We appreciate the work you have done and will consider ourselves in your debt," Libby replied.

"Thank you," Kelly said. "I'm afraid you'll need to find rooms for all four emissaries in that case, but I'd like to continue hosting Emperor Brynt."

"I've been dreaming about evicting Timba since the first day, but I didn't want to get on the wrong side of the Stryx," Crute said. He stretched out one of his lower arms for a bottle of the mediocre Vergallian wine Aluria had supplied, grabbed a corkscrew with the upper arm on the same side, and a glass with the lower arm on the other side. "This calls for a celebration."

"You didn't think of asking because you suffer from the same tunnel vision as the Cayl," Gwendolyn declared suddenly. The Gem ambassador had appeared to be lost in her own thoughts throughout the emergency meeting, but apparently she had been paying attention after all. "The four of you are so pleased with yourselves for not requesting help from the Stryx that you act like idiots. No, don't stop me," she said, as Kelly put a hand on her friend's shoulder to calm her. "If hosting those nasty emissaries failed to open the eyes of our colleagues, somebody should do it for them."

"Somebody whose species overthrew their rightful government with the help of the Stryx?" Aluria inquired.

183

"Oh, stuff it, Aluria," Gwendolyn replied. "Everybody here knows that the Stryx gifted us the money we needed to stage our revolution and buy back our genetic lines from the Farlings. Everybody here also knows that the only reason the Farlings didn't attack the Vergallians in retaliation for your rogue captain's raid on Farling Pharmaceutical's orbital three years ago was because you're part of the tunnel network."

Aluria sniffed loudly, but didn't contradict the angry clone.

"And you," the Gem ambassador continued, pointing at the Horten. "How much of your economy depends on laundering pirated goods, something the Stryx choose to ignore since you all swear that those Hortens are outcasts. And where would your precious networks be without the Stryxnet for real-time broadcasts," she added, turning on the giant bunny.

"We pay heavy fees for those services," the Grenouthian protested.

"And you charge even heavier fees for commercial time," Gwendolyn fired back. "And who, if not the Dollnick merchant princes, have accumulated one of the great fortunes in the galaxy without having to spend it all on military assets to prevent somebody bigger and meaner from coming and taking it away? So the Humans didn't develop their own faster-than-light drive. Big deal. At least they know better than to complain about their benefactors."

"Is there some point to your digression?" Ambassador Ortha inquired.

"I also believe that the behavior we're seeing from the guests is due to culture shock. If the Cayl are as paternal in the management of their empire as Ambassador McAllister suggests, the societies of their empire must have adapted to the approach. Maybe they simply don't know how to behave without Cayl supervision."

"Whereas the Stryx expect tunnel species to police themselves, but act with overwhelming force when it's required," Bork said. "It's as if both the Cayl and the Stryx run their domains like families, but with radically different parenting philosophies."

"The species of the Cayl Empire are a mismatch for the tunnel network," Srythlan boomed. "Our statisticians reached this conclusion based on the data, but they struggled to develop a theoretical model to explain the incompatibility."

"Then what are the Stryx up to?" the Grenouthian pondered out loud.

"And when is the catering going to arrive?" Czeros added.

"I thought she was taking care of it," Kelly said at the same time as Aluria.

The Frunge pushed away his wine in disgust, rose to his feet, and stalked out of the embassy. Bork shrugged and followed him, and the Chert vanished in the blink of an eye. The Verlock ambassador was much slower than the others, but once he began moving towards the exit, it was clear the meeting was concluded. Kelly offered to walk Gwendolyn back to the Gem embassy.

"I really am sick and tired of these scheming aliens," Gwendolyn said, clearly referring to the ambassadors who ostentatiously remained behind in the Vergallian embassy. "I'll bet Aluria even has food for just the four of them."

"You seem to be a bit on edge today," Kelly replied, trying not to sound critical. "Is something wrong?"

"Nothing is wrong, but I talked our options over with Mist and she decided on stasis," the Gem ambassador replied. "I think that Dorothy getting a boyfriend is what did it. I'll bring Mist back to our home world, she'll go to sleep, and when she wakes up in twelve or thirteen years, the first generation of cloned male Gems will be her age. I'm thinking of staying to help raise them."

"You mean you won't come back?"

"Probably not," Gwendolyn replied sadly. "I'll miss you and your family terribly, and I suppose I'll also miss Srythlan and Bork, even Czeros. But my sisters back home are trying to bring up a generation of boys without ever having seen a male of any species in their lives. At least I've babysat for Samuel and watched him growing up, and half of the sentients I deal with on the station are male. Compared to most of my people, I'm an expert in the opposite sex."

The only thing Kelly could think to offer in response was a going-away party.

Seventeen

"Have you developed a gold mask phobia?" Flazint asked Dorothy during a rare break in the action. The Frunge girl was wearing her hair vines straight up, which gave her the appearance of a child impersonating a tree in a school play. It was fortunate she had gone with the towering updo, because the two girls were working together behind the counter and there just wasn't room for a more elaborate horizontal arrangement.

"It's no big deal," Dorothy said. "I had a bit of a run-in with some of those Lood creeps on the Physics Ride last week."

"During your big date?" Flazint asked. "How was it?"

"It was nice. Well, we got into a fight with the Loods, and later, when I thought David was reaching for my hand on the way home, the dog decided to walk between us. But David invited me to dinner at Pub Haggis next weekend, and he's going to cook it himself."

"Wow, you're so lucky. Frunge guys don't enter the kitchen unless it's to drink out of the liquid fertilizer jar without using a cup."

"I've caught my dad and older brother doing that with the juice when they thought nobody was looking," Dorothy said in commiseration. "Anyway, David started shooting the Loods after they insulted me, even though he doesn't have an implant and couldn't tell what they were saying. And I sort of lost my temper and told them where I work."

"Oh, well. At least with the lost-and-found so busy now they won't catch you alone. I'm going to ask for a raise if the bots start bringing us baby Shugas or Nangors. Those aliens can't seem to leave a room without forgetting something."

"They're pretty lame," Dorothy agreed. "My mom says it's because the Cayl enforce strict rules against littering. When those aliens are at home, if they put something down and forgot it, they'd probably be fined, or eaten or something. Mom thinks that without a Cayl garrison to make their local authorities enforce the rules, the guests don't know how to behave."

"Excuse me," a Tzvim said, sidling up to the counter. "I seem to have mislaid a collection of Grenouthian documentaries I purchased earlier this morning."

"Holo-cubes or permanent storage?" the Frunge girl inquired.

"The collection was zapped onto the permanent memory of my—oh, no. This means I've lost my open ticket as well. Just look for a small, blue sphere with a slot in the center. I don't know if they'll let me back on the ship without it."

"Trust me. We'll do everything we can to see you on your way," the Frunge girl said, and rolled her eyes at Dorothy. "I'll check the overflow bins."

"I'll check the belt," Dorothy replied, as she began rummaging through the recently arrived objects under the intake end of the counter.

The system was bogging down under the sheer volume of stuff the bots had been finding abandoned since the guests arrived for the open house, necessitating double staffing. Fortunately, the aliens from the Cayl Empire were turning up at the lost-and-found almost as fast as the bots were bringing in new finds.

"I think I found it," Dorothy called out, holding up a blue sphere. "We just need to confirm it's yours and we'll release it."

"Of course it's mine," the Tzvim declared, making a grab for it over the counter and missing. "Where are you going with that?"

"Just to the end here, to put it through the scanner. The bots take a recording of every object where they find it, so the filing system can keep track of the items that haven't been moved to shelf storage."

Dorothy placed the blue sphere on the potter's wheel and gave it a gentle spin.

"Tzvim data locker and passenger transponder," the artificial voice intoned.

"There, you see?" the alien said aggressively. "Hand it over and I'll be on my way."

"Does the data locker contain a collection of Grenouthian documentaries purchased this morning?" Flazint asked the filing system.

"Data locker encrypted. Requesting assistance."

"If the sphere is damaged, you girls are going to pay for this," the Tzvim threatened.

"Decryption completed," a different voice said. "Checking contents."

"Is that you, Libby?" Dorothy asked.

"Yes," the Stryx librarian replied. "The documentaries recorded on this device are pre-release copies from the Grenouthian editing studio. Please wait while I review our security imaging and contact the studio to determine if the transaction was legitimate."

"I paid good currency for those documentaries," the alien protested. "Is it my responsibility to determine if the individual selling them had all of the proper authorizations?"

A hologram sprang into life above the 3D scanner's turntable, showing the turtle-backed alien in a corridor outside the main Grenouthian studio on the station. He held a bag out to a young bunny who accepted it, looked inside, and then withdrew a device similar to a flashlight from his pouch. The Tzvim held up the blue sphere and the Grenouthian zapped it with the data transfer device. In just a few seconds, the transaction was done and the pair split apart.

"You see?" the alien repeated querulously. "Perfectly legitimate trade."

"Awaiting confirmation from the studio," Libby said. The hologram continued to play, showing the Tzvim walking down the corridor to a lift tube. He entered the tube with the blue sphere still in his hand and gave the capsule his destination. Thirty seconds later he emerged in the all-species entertainment district, where he was met at the tube by another of his kind.

"Get it?" Geed asked bluntly.

"Got it," the alien confirmed, displaying the blue sphere.

"Celebration," the Tzvim emissary said, flashing her teeth.

The two Tzvim linked arms and strolled off in search of a drinking establishment near the Empire Convention Center. Libby speeded up the action, as the pair took corridor seats in front of a Dollnick bar and began ordering and quaffing glowing concoctions, one after another. Eventually, they bumped fists and headed off in their own directions, the blue sphere forgotten on the table, which was littered with the detritus of the celebration.

"Confirmation of an unauthorized transaction from the Grenouthian studio," Libby reported. "Wiping data. The studio will reclaim your payment from their former employee and forward it to the Grenouthian ambassador, who will return it to your emissary."

"This is illegal search and seizure," the Tzvim shouted, working himself into a passion. Dorothy and Flazint both backed away, and a pair of maintenance bots streaked into the room, as if summoned by rubbing a magic lamp.

"Take your sphere and go," one of the bots said in its mechanical voice.

The alien swept the blue sphere off the turntable, glared at the girls and the bots, and then stomped out.

"Thank you. Come again," Dorothy whispered to Flazint, and the two girls struggled to suppress their giggles. But they stopped almost immediately as a trio of gold-masked Loods strode in.

"You," the center figure in the trio proclaimed, pointing at the human girl. "Somebody in your Little Apple stole my purse. Return it immediately or face the consequences."

Relieved that it wasn't the young Lood from the Physics Ride, Dorothy put on her best customer service smile and tried to calm the agitated alien.

"I'm sorry to hear that, sir, but this is a lost-and-found and we don't receive stolen goods. Are you sure that your purse wasn't lost?"

"Look here," the Lood ordered imperiously, and for a moment Dorothy thought he was going to remove his mask. Instead, he held up a hand, wiggled his fingers to draw her eyes, and then put the hand in the pocket of his expensive cloak. His fingers continued right through the pocket to the outside of the garment. "Some scum sliced my pocket open and stole my purse while I was engaged in defending myself from ruffians."

"I see," Dorothy said, wondering where the two maintenance bots had gone. "But I'm afraid that means the thief has your purse, unless he removed the money and threw it away. Could you describe it?"

"Describe it?" the Lood shouted. "It looks like my purse!"

One of his companions intuited that this description was unlikely to move the process forward, and he removed his own purse from his cloak. It was made out of some sort of tanned skin or artificial substitute, and was tooled with a detailed hunting scene taking place in grasslands.

"His purse looks like this, except the animal being killed is a Shorinth rather than a Jalop," the companion explained helpfully.

"Black purse with a dying Shorinth," Dorothy repeated "We'll just take a look."

This time it was Flazint who located the purse in one of the overflow bins after several minutes of searching, during which time the girls struggled to ignore a running commentary on their inefficient methods offered by the angry Lood. The purse was heavy and made the sound of shifting coins as the Frunge girl placed it on the scanner's turntable.

"That's my purse!" the Lood declared, approaching the counter and reaching for it. He jerked his hand back in surprise as it encountered an invisible barrier that flashed yellow and delivered a shock.

192

"We have to check out all items," Dorothy said. "It's for your own protection, to prevent somebody dishonest from claiming it."

"Lood change purse and assorted coins from the Cayl Empire with a current exchange value of eighteen-hundred and seven Stryx creds," the cataloging system's voice announced.

"And it's mine," the Lood declared, rubbing his hand. "Are we through here?"

"Why would a thief return a full purse?" the helpful member of the trio asked.

"Don't forget we're talking about a human thief," the third Lood said. "They're all idiots."

"Libby?" Dorothy asked. "Do you have a holo of how the purse was stolen?"

"Retracing," Libby answered. A hologram appeared above the turntable, showing the purse lying on top of a mound of kebab sticks and food wrappers in the trash receptacle where a maintenance bot had found it. The scene seemed to jerk around for a moment as the Stryx librarian matched the bot's recovery record against images from the security system, then a positive lock was achieved.

"Can you start a minute before the loss?" Flazint asked.

Three cloaked figures, viewed from above and behind, popped into existence near the trash receptacle. They were engaged in a loud dispute with a woman wearing an apron.

"Do you think because I'm human I just fell off the turnip cart?" the angry woman asked in English. "That's three breakfast specials for nine creds total, and you're lucky I don't charge you for that bottle of vinegar you dumped all over your toast."

"And this is a ten-cred coin," came the voice of one of the Loods. He held out the tiny copper-colored disc they were arguing over. "It includes a tip for your fine service."

"It's not ten Stryx creds," the woman said. She lifted her arm and waved a large ladle at the aliens. "I'm not afraid of anybody who has to hide behind a mask, so fork over something that my register likes and I'll make the change."

"Watch out," one of the Loods shouted. "She's got a Frazzleopper."

All three aliens drew long knives out of back scabbards concealed under their cloaks, and in bringing them around their bodies, one of the Loods sliced through the cloak of his neighbor. The change purse dropped out into the trash can.

Several large men pushed into the scene, brandishing kitchen knives and meat cleavers. At their head Dorothy recognized Ian, who was wielding a Claymore that usually hung over the bar in Pub Haggis. David followed behind his employer with an iron frying pan.

One of the Loods reached for his mask but another one knocked his hand away. "Don't," he admonished. "There's too many of them. We'd never make it out of here."

"That's nine creds you owe me," the woman repeated, waving her ladle under the middle Lood's nose.

"Of course, it was just a misunderstanding," the alien gritted out. "Z'harp. You changed some money with that Thark, didn't you?"

"Cheapskate," muttered Z'harp, who the girls now recognized as the helpful one of the trio. He returned his knife to its sheath and dug out a ten-cred piece from his purse. "Your kitchen implement looks very much like a neural overload device used by Shuga cutthroats," he said apologetically to the woman. The hologram blinked out.

194

"Here you go, sir," Flazint said, handing the purse to its owner.

The Lood accepted the purse angrily and stuffed it in the pocket of his cloak, where it immediately dropped through the slit and landed on his foot. He glared wordlessly at the companion who had cut open the cloak with his sloppy knife-play, and that Lood quickly bent to retrieve the purse.

"Pay the fee, Z'harp," the leader said. "Z'ding is taking me shopping for a new cloak." He strode out of the lost-and-found with an unhappy companion in tow.

"How much will my older brother's error cost me this time?" Z'harp asked in a resigned voice.

"There's no fee," Flazint told the Lood. "Some sentients tip, but it's not mandatory."

Z'harp reached into the change purse with the scene of the Jalop hunt and pulled out a five-cred piece, which he placed on the counter. Then he looked at it and hesitated, as if he had mistaken the coin for one of smaller value. Z'harp cleared his throat nervously.

"Would it be possible to purchase a copy of that hologram from the breakfast place?" he asked.

"It's free with the tip if you have your own storage device," Flazint told him, much to Dorothy's surprise. The Frunge girl added an aside for her co-worker. "People come back and ask for the security holograms all the time, usually friends and family members. The high resolution version is only available for a couple of days, though. I guess even the Stryx run out of storage space eventually."

When Flazint turned back to the Lood, he was proffering his knife, held by the tip.

"My personal storage unit is in the handle," he said. "Can your device access it?"

195

"Sure, it works with everything," Flazint asserted. She accepted the knife, placed it on the turntable, and requested a copy of the confrontation. The hologram they had just watched played again, but at twenty times the speed. In a few seconds, the transfer was over.

"Thank you," Z'harp said. "We're not all, uh, you know."

"No species is," Flazint answered philosophically, spinning the Lood's five-cred piece on the counter. "Come again any time."

"Thank you," Dorothy added.

"There's our lunch money," Flazint said as soon as the Lood took his leave. "Are you feeling adventurous?"

"Humans can't tolerate much cross-species food," Dorothy admitted. "Just some of the grains and vegetables, and you guys don't eat grains."

"We could get something from the Little Apple," the Frunge girl offered generously. "Sometimes my family orders a pizza special without the dough, but you could get it under your half."

"Great! We've got plenty in the tip jar to splurge on delivery."

"Oh, I forgot. Somebody will have to go for it," Flazint said. "They won't take a crustless order unless you show up in person. I guess they have trouble with pranks."

"You go ahead," Dorothy said. "Business seems to have slowed down a bit, probably another big party in the hotel district."

"If things get busy, just ping me, and I'll come back as soon as they take the order. Otherwise, I shouldn't be more than twenty minutes."

Dorothy decided to use the time to familiarize herself with the objects in the overflow bins behind the counter, which were effectively blocking the bottom row of shelves. She was puzzling over a device that looked like a cross between a tiny folding chair and a pair of headphones when the Lood returned.

"Is something wrong with the recording, Z'harp?" she inquired.

"I know nothing of a recording," the Lood replied, reaching for his mask.

Dorothy's blood ran cold when she recognized the voice of the young Lord Z'fark from the Physics Ride. She blanched in horror as the Lood removed his mask, revealing a lidless third eye in the middle of his forehead which glowed with a malignant inner light.

"I am very happy to encounter you again, Dorothy McAllister," Z'fark said in a honeyed voice. "Wouldn't you like to come with me and see my ship?"

As much as she was disgusted by the third eye, Dorothy felt compelled to stare directly at it, and her mind began to feel oddly blank. Wasn't there somebody she was supposed to call or something she was supposed to do? All of her thoughts seemed to be pulled towards that awful eye, and then she found herself wondering why she had never seen the inside of a Lood ship. The light emitted by the eye grew brighter and brighter, and without thinking, she raised a hand to try to keep it from blinding her.

"Witch!" the Lood cried in fear. He dropped to his knees, turning away and replacing his gold mask at the same time. "Forgive me, witch. How could I know you were appearing in the form of a lowly Human?"

Dorothy blinked as her own thoughts rushed back and her vision returned to normal. The first thing she saw was her hand raised before her face, the black bracelet displayed prominently on her wrist where the sleeve of her blouse had fallen back. The runes engraved in the strange metal glowed like lava.

"Get out!" she screamed at the Lood, who half stumbled, half crawled to the exit and disappeared. Dorothy sank down on the floor, her arms around her knees, taken by a sudden fit of trembling. It took her a minute just to catch her breath enough to say, "Libby?"

"Yes, Dorothy," the station librarian replied. "Your adrenalin levels are highly elevated and they'll return to normal faster if you walk back and forth behind the counter. I'll keep the doors closed until Flazint returns. Our careless open house guests can come back later."

"He was going to make me go with him," Dorothy whispered. "Why didn't you explain that the bracelet would protect me?"

"The Lood's fear of what the bracelet represents is what protected you," the Stryx librarian explained. "If I had sent a bot to escort him off the station, he might have tried something again in the future, maybe finding you in some place where you'd truly be alone. Some sentients will go to extreme lengths to avenge an imagined injury. This way, he'll want to keep as far away from you as possible as long as he lives, and he'll tell his friends that human girls can be dangerous."

Dorothy struggled to her feet and began to walk shakily back and forth behind the counter. After a few minutes, her heart rate began to slow and she started thinking about practical things.

"Libby?"

"Yes, Dorothy."

"Don't tell my parents about this. They might get all weird about my going out alone on dates with David."

Eighteen

"Thank you for keeping the hostages entertained all morning," Pava said to her mother-in-law. "I hope you've given them a chance to win back some of their losses."

"The hostages really have a gift for this game." The Dowager Empress looked up from her tiles and peered at the Union Station delegation. "The funny-looking one almost took the deal from me."

"It's very similar to the Korean version of Mahjong that my husband taught me on our honeymoon," Lynx replied. After weeks of daily exposure to the emperor's mother, she had developed a soft spot for the blunt old Cayl. "We used to play with the ship controller as a third."

"And I learned the traditional four-handed version playing in the tea house at the Shuk during slow hours." Brinda swapped a tile from the front to the back of her double row and added, "Don't ever get into a game with a Stryx."

"Would you be referring to young Jeeves, the Stryx who arranged for the hostage swap?" the Dowager Empress asked. She played a tile inscribed with an ancient Cayl character, making clear she had no intention of letting the humans go before the hand was finished. "I thought he caught on to the strategy a little too quickly for somebody who claimed never to have played before."

"I'm still a little fuzzy on what all the lizard pieces mean," Woojin said.

"They're bonus pieces, think of them as doublers," the Dowager Empress explained. "Speaking of which, I have four of them, and thanks to your discard, I also seem to have made Cryan Hah again. Shall I total up the points?"

"When you said we have a gift for the game, I think you meant we're a gift TO your game," Lynx grumbled good-naturedly.

"Were you involved in the hostage negotiations, Kiki?" Woojin asked. He was the only one who had taken the emperor's mother at her word when she told them to ignore her official title.

"Oh, yes," the Dowager Empress replied. "It's one of my few official duties, along with choosing a new emperor should my Brynt not return or do something equally unacceptable. I specifically requested of Stryx Jeeves that he select hostages with an aptitude for Cryan Hah to console me for my son's absence."

"I should have known he wasn't serious about holding an auction for you when he didn't draw up a draft contract," Brinda said. "Wouldn't it have been more conventional to ask for a hostage of equal value?"

"And where would the Stryx have obtained one of those?" the old Cayl asked imperiously. "I'd have to request the population of an entire world to get within clawing distance of equal value for my Brynt, and then my daughter-in-law would have to feed them all."

"I guess we don't really have anybody of the emperor's rank and power in the tunnel network species, but you might keep Jeeves next time," Lynx suggested.

"Keep a Stryx?" The Dowager Empress cackled as she began stacking the Cryan Hah tiles back in their plain wooden case. "Stryx are pretty indestructible, if you haven't noticed, which hardly makes them good hostage material. And even if we did catch his robotic puppet with its guard down, their minds aren't locked into the same physical space. The Stryx went multi-dimensional long before our predecessor species came out of the forests and began damming streams."

A number of Cayl cubs barreled into the room, batting an inky black ball back and forth between them. Every time the ball contacted a surface, it rebounded at an unexpected angle, as if it was rapidly spinning. When the ball shot past the table, Woojin made a dive for it, but it changed course midair to avoid his grasp. The Cayl cubs found this hilarious and fell on the floor alongside him, flailing their limbs in a display of mirth.

"I see males really are the same everywhere," the Dowager Empress commented. She finished packing the Cryan Hah pieces back into their case and sighed. "I'm afraid I've forgotten which one of you he belongs to."

"Me," Lynx said, getting up from the table and helping her husband off the deck.

"This morning I received a message from your Jeeves that the open house on Union Station is winding down and my Brynt will be coming home soon," the empress said. "I'm sorry I've been so tied up with babysitting, it can't have been a very nice hostage experience for you. If you don't mind being in an airship with children, I'd like to take you on a tour of our surroundings."

"That sounds wonderful," Brinda said, rising from the table. "I've been looking forward to seeing more of your planet. But didn't you tell the four ambassadors at the state dinner that hostage protocols prevent you from allowing us outside of the palace grounds?"

"They seemed so anxious to involve you in a fatal sight-seeing accident that I thought it wise to nip that idea in the bud," Pava said. "The ambassadors aren't the most original thinkers, but they are persistent, and I didn't want to expose you to any unnecessary danger."

"But we were told that the Cayl never lie to guests," Lynx objected, immediately wishing she had chosen a more diplomatic way to express the thought.

"I'm sure you can see how it's useful to us for our guests to believe that," the Dowager Empress replied with a wink. "Now it's time for my nap, so please make sure you have all of the cubs with you before you go out."

The empress herded the young Cayl out of the game room before her, and then led the humans through a seemingly endless series of twisty passages to an armored door. There she turned around and faced the three, an unusually serious expression on her normally cheerful face.

"Can I trust you to keep a secret?"

"We're professional spies," Woojin said, placing his arm around Lynx's shoulders. "It depends who you want the secret kept from."

"Good answer." Pava's features relaxed into a bearish smile. "I'm not even sure why I asked that since I'm sure your Stryx do the same thing all the time. It's just that I'm planning to bring you to the alien market later today, and it would be best not to mention this to any of the vendors."

"Mum's the word," Woojin promised, and the two women nodded their agreement.

The empress said something their implants didn't translate, and the door swung upwards, allowing them into a laboratory that would have looked at home in a twentieth century horror film. Oddly shaped containers of some transparent substance held brightly colored fluids that moved between vessels through looping spirals of tubing. Electrical discharges leapt between shiny metal balls in continuous arcs, and a rhythmic mechanical sound like a belt running over a flywheel provided the audio ambiance.

"Are you running an experiment?" Lynx asked the empress.

"None of this was here the last time I came, so it must be some kind of art project that the youngsters are working on. The device I wanted to show you is in the corner."

Pava brought the humans over to a garishly painted statue of a mythical looking creature with two sets of wings. It was equipped with a single button on the top of its head, and a slot above a silver semi-hemispherical basin under the belly.

"Should I press the button?" Brinda asked, finding herself the closest to the device. The empress nodded, so the younger Hadad sister reached over and pushed the blue button with her forefinger. The wings flapped metallically a few times, there was a sound like a metal washer rolling down a long track, and then a gold coin popped out of the slot and clanged into the catch basin.

"It's a mechanical bank," Brinda exclaimed. "We've sold a few antique ones on the auction circuit. They used to be very popular with humans. This is the largest one I've ever seen, though come to think of it, the mechanism is usually designed to accept coins, not disgorge them."

"Make some more," the empress encouraged her. "Five for each of you should be plenty. A gold imperial goes a long way in the alien market."

Brinda pressed the button four times in rapid succession, the creature flapped its metal wings steadily, and four more coins clanged out. "You guys try it," she suggested to her companions.

As Woojin stepped forward and pressed the button, Lynx turned to the empress and asked, "Did you mean to imply that this little machine is minting these coins freshly for us?"

"It doesn't mint them in the sense I think you mean, starting with gold bullion and shaping coins using a stamping or liquid molding process. The materializer uses a neutron collider on the upper deck to create a soup of gold atoms, after which they're formed into coins with manipulator fields. I'd show you the materialization phase, but the gamma radiation levels require that it be heavily shielded. I'm sure you know that most of the gold in the universe comes from collisions between neutron stars, and although our Golden Goose is a pale imitation of nature, it helps me keep up with household expenses."

"Do, uh, all the Cayl make their own gold?" Lynx asked.

"Oh, no. It's a simple process but very energy intensive, and it would hardly be practical if the ship's main engines hadn't remained intact. I know the palace doesn't make a very good impression on visitors, but there are some advantages to having access to warship-scale energy piles and equipment, not to mention the nearly unlimited closet space. Brynt frowns on my using our Golden Goose because he'd rather I sell more art forgeries, but I can hardly send the three of you out peddling my grand-children's pottery for pocket money."

Lynx took her turn at making gold coins, and then the empress led them out of the room and up a different passage, away from the direction from which they'd arrived.

"I told my eldest granddaughter to gather up the cubs and meet us at the imperial yacht," Pava said, guiding the humans through a particularly narrow point in the corridor where the bulkheads had been crushed in from both sides. "The deck can get a bit slippery up ahead because Brynt keeps putting off doing something about the leaks. I don't often come this way."

"I don't get it," Lynx muttered to her husband as the water began soaking through her socks. "They have a machine that makes gold out of, whatever, and she won't hire somebody to repair the roof?"

"Hull," Woojin corrected her. "Why don't you just ask her?"

"I will," Lynx declared, sloshing ahead. "Empress? Do you mind if I ask why you don't just make some gold and pay somebody to repair the hull leaks?"

"The ship's skin is a special alloy that can only be welded in a vacuum," Pava replied. "All of our naval construction is done in orbital shipyards, of course, and nobody can justify the resources necessary to launch the palace into orbit for repairs. I think the real reason Brynt procrastinates gluing a tarp over this section of the hull is because the hounds like having a place inside to splash around and get a drink."

The corridor opened up into a large bay that was littered with sections of various types of vessels that were either undergoing repairs or being torn down for parts. Directly in their path was a craft that looked very much like it had been sawed in half along its length and then abandoned. A dozen heads popped up over the side and peered down at the new arrivals.

"Hurry up, Grams. The cubs are driving me crazy!" shouted a young Cayl. The humans recognized her as the granddaughter who had interrupted the state dinner to tell the empress about the cub with the stomach complaint. She was visible just long enough to deliver this message before she disappeared under a pile of playful young siblings and cousins.

"They look pretty excited about getting out," Lynx said. "Is the yacht on the other side of that wreck?"

"Not exactly," the empress replied, leading them to a ramp that penetrated the hull of the half-ship. "It doesn't look like much, but I assure you it's entirely airworthy. One of the previous emperors made it out of an old lifeboat because he wanted an atmospheric craft with a lot of power for towing, and of course, the palace is crammed with old lifeboats. He liked fresh air so he cut off half the hull, but he never got around to adding a convertible top for if it rains."

A section of the palace hull above their heads began to retract and the yacht lifted smoothly into the air. The craft soared through the opening as soon as there was sufficient clearance, lightly scraping the side as the cubs pulled back their noses.

"Is the, uh, yacht's captain a Cayl warrior?" Lynx asked nervously, as the vessel gained altitude and speed. A breeze was felt throughout the open boat, and the cubs and the hounds competed for space to hang their heads over the prow, smiling as the strong wind flattened their hair and cooled their tongues.

"My granddaughter, Krey, is flying," the empress said, indicating the young Cayl near the rear of the open cockpit. The medium-size female had one paw on a joystick, but she appeared to be looking down, rather than forward. "Would you like to try? I'm sure she'd be willing to teach you."

206

Over Woojin's vociferous protest that Krey was doing just fine, Pava led the hostages to the stern. Halfway there, Lynx made the mistake of looking down and saw nothing but the ground rushing past. She grabbed her husband's arm and choked back a scream.

"Is this section of the hull transparent, or are we held up by some sort of retention field?" Woojin asked the empress.

"It's part of the original lifeboat hull, to allow the passengers to see out. All Cayl ships use transparent materials for sections of the hull. Oh, look at those boys trying to show off for our Krey."

Far below them, the humans saw a pack of Cayl streaking across the fields on all fours to keep up with the imperial yacht. They seemed to collide with each other whenever the opportunity arose, leading to spectacular tumbles. At one point, as the young males approached a riverbank that looked more like a cliff, Krey took both of her hands off the joystick tiller to cover her eyes.

"If you don't want to see them crack their skulls open, fly over the level fields until you wear them out," the empress told her granddaughter in irritation.

The girl opened one eye and banked the air yacht sharply to starboard, without crossing the river. A couple of the young cubs hanging over the side were caught unawares, and they might have gone overboard if their guardian hounds hadn't chomped down on the loose fur behind their necks, hauling them back. Below the half-lifeboat, a couple of the racing males failed to make the corner and skidded over the embankment for a steep drop into the river.

"Aren't those boys risking serious injury?" Brinda asked.

"It's part of their nature," the empress replied. "Your Stryx tell us that our species is one of the few they've encountered with such an uneven distribution of males and females at birth. We start with twice as many males born as females, but by the time they reach maturity, the ratio is roughly equal. Our boys are utterly reckless."

"But you're supposed to be one of the most advanced biological species in the galaxy," Lynx protested. "Can't you fix it?"

"Supposed to be?" Pava repeated. "Don't let my mother-in-law hear you say that. Of course we can interfere with the natural rhythms of our bodies and produce an equal number of males and females, but unless we sedated all of the males or established plural marriage, half of the females would die old maids. Our ancestors tried all three solutions, but it just made everybody unhappy, even the parents who were spared the deaths of their sons. In the end, we developed rituals to help us deal with the short, happy lives of so many of our offspring, and stopped warring with our nature."

"So with all the science and technology you possess, one of those males showing off for your granddaughter could collide with a tree or a rock and die?"

"It happens frequently on mating runs," the empress said. She gazed down through the transparent section of hull at the pack of males, which quickly was falling behind. "I doubt any of that lot have the stamina to catch my Krey when she's ready for marriage. She has fast genes from both sides of the family."

"And the parents of the boys won't object over their marrying into the imperial family as your mother did?" Lynx asked.

"Imperial succession is strictly through the male line, so there's no onus on marrying an imperial daughter or granddaughter," the empress explained. "In addition to a daughter, I had three sons, two of whom survived. Krey is the firstborn daughter of my elder son, Bwine."

"Ah, I think I finally have it all straight now," Woojin said. "Bwine is the one Kiki told us she would appoint to replace Brynt if he persists with dissolving the empire."

"What are you talking about?" the empress gasped, grabbing for a railing to hold herself steady. "Brynt has two younger brothers, Lang and Ruke. They're both in line to succeed."

"Kiki said she's had enough of being Dowager Empress to last a lifetime, and that the empire obviously needs young blood. Wait. If Bwine is your son, wouldn't that make you the next Dowager Empress?"

"Do you have the ability to contact the Stryx science ship that brought you here, or do we have to return to the palace?" the empress asked urgently. "I need to send Brynt a message."

"Stryx Vrine said we could get through from anywhere with these," Woojin said, offering the empress his necklace.

Pava held the empty locket in front of her mouth and spoke into the opening. "Stryx?"

"Yes, Empress," Vrine replied. "I hope no harm has come to the hostages."

"Nothing like that, Stryx. I need to get a message to my husband. I'm not requesting your extra-dimensional services, just that you send something through your tunnel next time it's open."

"What's the message, Empress?"

"Brynt. Your mother plans to replace you with Bwine. Pava."

209

Nineteen

"Something's wrong," Kelly asserted, looking around Mac's Bones as if she expected to see storm clouds threatening below the atmosphere retention field. "Where's Beowulf?"

"He ran off by himself after breakfast," Samuel said, dancing around his mother with an invisible partner. "I wanted to go with him, but he beat me to the lift tube, and then it wouldn't tell me where he went."

"He must have smelled something through the ventilation system," Joe said. "It used to happen from time to time before he was reincarnated. Usually, he'd come back and throw up all over the place, so it's probably food-related."

"Do you have to do that, Samuel?' Kelly asked her son. "Isn't practicing five days a week enough?"

"The Vergallians practice every day," the boy told her. "They're the best dancers."

"A warrior should know how to dance," the Cayl emperor said encouragingly. "Dancing helps develop good footwork for sword fighting."

"I still feel like something funny is going on, and it's not the dog running off," Kelly said.

Samuel grinned to himself and went on dancing. He'd noticed that his mother usually deferred to the Cayl, which was great, because the emperor almost always took the boy's side. The two exceptions were lima beans and bedtime, both of which the emperor insisted were important for growing warriors.

"You're always looking for problems on Saturdays," Joe said. "It's because you aren't getting embassy pings every minute."

"That's it!" Kelly declared. "It's too quiet. How come I'm not getting any complaints from the merchants in the Little Apple or the Shuk? Why aren't any of the ambassadors pushing me for another emergency meeting?"

"Good morning," a familiar young man called as he approached the patio. "Bob Steelforth, Galactic Free Press."

"It's the weekend, Bob," Joe pointed out.

"I'm working," the reporter said. "My editor sent me to get your thoughts about the Cayl police force that the Stryx hired. I'm sorry for bursting in on a Saturday morning like this."

"What?" Kelly exclaimed. She turned to Brynt to see his reaction.

"I'm sorry for coming on a Saturday," Bob repeated, speaking louder and slower for the old folks.

"I meant, what's this about a Cayl police force?" Kelly said in exasperation.

"Oh. The Stryx hired a whole bunch of Cayl from somewhere. They have dogs that look just like yours, maybe a bit smaller."

"That's not possible," Brynt protested. "I sent my shuttle back through the temporary tunnel."

"Maybe some of them went freelance," Bob said, showing off his new mastery of reporting jargon. "All I know is that the Little Apple and the Shuk deck are normal again, and when I stopped at the entertainment district on my way here, you could actually hear the music over the yelling for the first time since all those guests arrived."

"What's going on, Libby?" the EarthCent ambassador subvoced.

"Jeeves talked Gryph into asking a few of the second generation Stryx to divert their science ships to some of the closer Cayl holdings to hire temporary help," Libby replied privately.

"Without telling the emperor?"

"Jeeves said that the emperor seemed a bit touchy on the subject of colonists. We're talking about the expeditions the Cayl sent out over the past few million years to settle the far reaches of the galaxy. The farther from the Cayl Empire, the closer to us."

"Emperor?" Kelly asked politely, interrupting his interrogation of the young reporter, who didn't have any of the answers the Cayl was seeking. "I'm told that the Stryx brought in some of your people from the colonizing groups you sent out long ago. I guess Jeeves had something to do with it."

"I should have foreseen this outcome after we talked about colonists at the poker game. Will you take me to visit one of the places these Cayl are policing?"

"Right away," Kelly replied. "I'll ping you if we won't be back for lunch, Joe. I'm taking him to the Shuk."

By the time they reached the lift tube, the young reporter managed to convince the EarthCent ambassador and the Cayl emperor to let him tag along. Brynt gave Steelforth a brief rundown on the Cayl colonization movement, which left the reporter so confused that Kelly had to explain the Cayl's singular conceptions of honor and respect. In the back of her mind, she registered that the one-minute ride to the Shuk stretched out to at least ten minutes, but there would be time to ask Libby about that later.

"So once or twice every million years, you finish construction of a colonization fleet, load it up with a quarter of your population and treasure, and send them off never to be heard from again," Steelforth recapped, checking the notes on his tab.

"There's no treasure in the sense you mean," Brynt informed him. "We make copies of our libraries and share our laboratory equipment, along with all the usual things colonists would take. We divide everything equally."

"And you don't even try to pick up their communications traffic?"

"We intentionally don't monitor the volumes of space our expeditions have selected for colonization, and I'm sure they avoid listening in on us for the same reason," the Cayl explained. "It would be a violation of their privacy."

The young reporter looked at Kelly helplessly. "I don't get it," he said. "Am I asking the wrong questions?"

"You're doing fine," Kelly told him. "It's just that the Cayl are aliens and they don't think like us. You weren't around ten years ago for the Kasilian auction, but there's an example of an advanced species which had to let its population collapse and give away everything they owned to regain their youthful optimism and a chance to start over."

The capsule door finally slid open, and contrary to his usual deferential attitude as a guest, the Cayl was the first one out. The market seemed completely normal, which immediately struck Kelly as suspicious, since it had been anything but since the open house began.

"This way," she suggested, leading the Cayl and the reporter towards Kitchen Kitsch, in the human section.

They hadn't gone twenty paces before a giant dog, which looked amazingly like Beowulf, trotted up and growled at a group of Shugas shopping at a Gem collectibles booth. One by one, the aliens emptied their pouches of the knickknacks they'd been shoplifting.

"I recognize the Cayl by the paw print of his dog," Brynt muttered. "Just a saying," he added, when Kelly gave him a questioning look.

As they continued through the Gem booths toward the human section, they found themselves approaching another, slightly smaller Cayl hound, which was blocking the path of a Tzvim. The dog sat upright on its haunches and had placed a paw in the middle of the alien's turtle-shell chest, like a crossing guard stopping a rambunctious child from running into traffic.

"I didn't do anything," the Tzvim protested.

The dog shook its head, almost sadly, Kelly thought, and didn't remove the paw.

"But they're Dollnicks," the turtle-like alien tried again. "They do stuff like that to other species all the time."

The dog pulled back its upper lip, revealing a display of enamel that would make a shark jealous.

"I'll buy it back," the Tzvim offered in defeat. The dog dropped its paw and indicated the way back to the Dollnick section by raising its muzzle. The two set off, the Cayl hound obviously in charge.

"Your dogs really seem to have a way with your empire's species," Kelly commented.

"We couldn't have run the empire so long without them," the emperor replied. "Supervising the behavior of adults isn't a job I would wish on my worst enemy, but our hounds were bred to the task and they actually enjoy it.

214

Every world in our empire has a Cayl garrison and a large contingent of hounds to watch over the local authorities."

"So you police the authorities rather than the people?" Steelforth asked.

"Of course," the emperor replied. "Back in ancient times, when our empire only included a dozen stars, we determined that the most effective system was to leave the existing governments in place on the worlds we conquered. All of our occupation efforts went into forcing the local leaders to obey their own laws, with a few additions that we impose on all of our worlds for fairness. Once the system is up and running, it tends to be self-perpetuating, and we've never had a serious problem with revolts."

"Here we are," Kelly said, as they crossed into the human section near Kitchen Kitsch. "I don't see any shimmering around the booth, so Peter must have stopped paying for the Stryx security field he told me he rented."

The Cayl emperor stopped and sniffed the air with an intensity that rivaled Beowulf on a visit to the Little Apple, and then he started off suddenly between a confectionery shop and a linens seller. Kelly and the reporter had to break stride several times to keep up with Brynt, and Beowulf emerged from a side passage and began trotting along with them.

Suddenly, they found themselves face-to-face with a pair of Cayl warriors wearing green tunics with a Union Station emblem. The two Cayl stared at Brynt in shock, and Kelly noticed that their eyes were not on the emperor's face, but the heavy gold chain around his neck. Then their knees just seemed to buckle and they prostrated themselves on the deck.

"Rise, rise," the emperor ordered, but they stayed on the deck, one wrapping his arms over his ears. Brynt strode forward, bent down, and grabbed each by a wrist. Then he straightened up rapidly, like a weight-lifter completing a competition lift. One of the strange Cayl found his feet, but the other curled up in the fetal position and dangled by his wrist.

"Is he dead?" the young reporter whispered to Kelly, all the while tapping frantically on his reporter's tab.

"I think he's embarrassed," Kelly whispered back.

"Stop that!" the emperor ordered, shaking the suspended Cayl in an impressive display of strength. "Put your feet down and stand up like a warrior."

"We didn't know any First Cayl were here, much less the First among Firsts," stuttered the other warrior, who had recovered more quickly from the shock of the meeting. "We never would have accepted the job from the Stryx had we known you were in charge here."

The emperor let go of the wrist of the second Cayl and turned to reply to the speaker. In that instant, the newly released warrior drew a device from his belt that looked like a hilt without a sword, and stretched his arm out in front of his body. As Kelly watched in shock, a fiery blade of red light leapt from the hilt, pointing towards the holder's own chest.

"Accept my life to atone for the offense given by our column," the warrior declared, but before he could impale himself or fall forward on the blade, a massive pair of jaws closed on his wrist, snapping the bones like tinder. The blade disappeared as the hilt fell to the deck.

"Good dog," the emperor said to Beowulf, who was in fact astounded by his own deed, never having bitten anybody before. Beowulf wasn't really sure what it was all about, but he didn't like seeing a weapon pulled in front of his ambassador or the emperor, even if it was pointed the wrong way. Kelly would have sworn the dog gave her a wink before resuming a fierce expression and staring at his victim. The pain of a broken wrist seemed to be just what the doctor had ordered. The warrior's stoicism took over and he stood at attention.

"Both of you stop acting ridiculous," Brynt barked. "You're Cayl warriors doing a job and that's what your honor depends on. This station belongs to the Stryx, and I am merely here as a guest while representatives of the species from our empire attend the open house. The outrageous behavior of our citizens has been a great shame for me, but as a guest, I couldn't think of interfering with the Stryx administration."

"Yes, First," the two warriors said, though Kelly suspected it was the only acceptable reply the Cayl had for any pronouncement of their emperor.

"How many of you are on the station?" the emperor followed up.

"One column from Second Cayl and one column from Fourth Cayl," the uninjured warrior answered promptly. "It was a great shock meeting our brothers here, and the Stryx tell us that columns from Third, Fifth and Sixth Cayl are on the way."

"You," the emperor growled, turning to the injured Cayl. "Go to the column surgeon and have your wrist repaired."

"It's fine," the Cayl protested. "I'm perfectly capable of carrying out my duties."

"I heard the bones crack and you're dripping blood on the floor," the emperor said, but he relented after taking a moment to put himself in the warrior's shoes. "At least wrap something around it so you don't make a mess."

"Yes, First," the warrior snapped in response.

"Inform your column leader that I will visit your field headquarters this evening," the emperor continued. "As the two of you are the only colony Cayl I have ever met, I request you join me after your shift in a meal to honor the occasion."

"Yes, First," the pair responded.

The emperor gave them a stiff head nod of dismissal, but stopped them with a question when they started to turn away. "Which colony are you from?"

"Fourth Cayl, First," the more loquacious of the pair replied.

"Carry on," Brynt said.

"Will he be all right?" Kelly asked as the injured Cayl moved off, his wrist tucked into his armpit to prevent dripping.

"He's a Cayl warrior," the emperor replied. "I can't understand why the Stryx would hire five columns for this job. A dozen warriors and their dogs would have been ample."

"How many warriors in a column," the reporter asked, his fingers poised over his tab.

"Two-hundred and eight," the emperor replied absently, watching the backs of the departing Cayl. "That includes the surgeon, cook, and command staff. It's the standard size of a planetary garrison."

"Do you mean you've been keeping the peace in your empire with just a couple hundred warriors per planet?" Kelly asked in astonishment. Beowulf gave a sharp bark. "And their Cayl hounds?"

Brynt absentmindedly scratched the giant dog behind the ears as he sniffed the air. "Warriors need to eat, as do their dogs. At the prices the planetary governments charge for hosting the garrisons, we can't afford to make them

218

larger. Besides, the ground troops are just there to keep the local politicians honest. Our strength is our warriors, but our weapon is our fleet."

A strangely delicate Cayl hound hurtled around the corner with her nose to the deck and then skidded to a halt. Beowulf made sure she was watching him, and then he blatantly knocked back the flap of one of the emperor's belt pouches with his nose and fished out a couple of biscuits with his tongue.

"Don't get into the habit," Brynt remonstrated.

Beowulf scraped one of the biscuits off his tongue against his front teeth so it dropped to the deck. Next he slid it over to the pretty hound with his nose. She picked it up, crunched, and eyed him speculatively. Then she trotted off, Beowulf following on her heels.

Twenty

The going-away party for Mist and Gwen might have turned out to be a depressing event if it had been limited to family and friends. Instead, both clones insisted that the McAllisters combine it with an end-of-open-house celebration, which brought the aliens out of the woodwork. Not only did Aluria put in a showing, but she offered grudging applause when Samuel and Vivian gave a brief demonstration of Vergallian ballroom dancing. After that, Thomas and Chance did an Argentinean tango interpretation which left no doubt that the artificial people had officially become a couple.

A lull in the dancing followed while the females of various species waited for the males to absorb enough alcohol to feel the rhythm. Dorothy and Mist dragged the unfortunate David onto the improvised dance floor and began teaching him the basics of couple dancing, while simultaneously making him feel like a third wheel by reminiscing about their best times together before he came into the picture.

"I wish they'd stop telling me that I wasn't so bad for a clone," Gwen complained half-jokingly to Kelly. The EarthCent ambassador had insisted that the Gem ambassador stand with her in front of the drinks table, forcing all of the other ambassadors in attendance to say something civil if they wanted to be served.

"A decade ago they would have snubbed both of us," Kelly pointed out. "Besides, did you hear what the Fillinduck said to me?"

"You don't smell as bad as he'd been warned." Gwen laughed. "At least now we know why he kept skipping the emergency meetings. Then he got a pint of beer from Joe and drank it like it was water. He's been standing over there staring at his stomach and hiccupping ever since."

"As long as he keeps it down," Kelly responded philosophically. "You're going to miss some exciting times if those Cayl Empire species decide to sign up for the tunnel network."

"We'll find out soon enough. According to Gem Today, the Stryx will be making an announcement any time."

"Gem Today covers events on Union Station? I didn't even know they had foreign correspondents."

"I helped them negotiate a deal for a syndication feed from the Galactic Free Press. Chastity isn't looking to go into competition with the Grenouthians on covering news for all of the species, but a lot of the stories from Stryx stations affect everybody. Oh, look at Chastity dancing with her husband. They're almost as good as Chance and Thomas."

"I have to admit that Marcus is a great teacher." Kelly checked over both shoulders and lowered her voice. "The truth is, I wasn't that happy when Samuel started training for ballroom dancing with Blythe's daughter. It just seemed like too big of a time commitment at their age, though sometimes I think that Vivian is six going on sixteen. But Chastity's husband makes it fun for them, and if I had to choose for my son between three hours a day of dancing and three hours a day of playing holo-war games, I'd take dancing every time."

221

"Ah, my favorite species," Walter declared, approaching the pair of ambassadors. As the city desk editor for Union Station, he'd been the point man for the Gem syndication negotiations. "May I request the next dance?" He theatrically extended his hand to Gwen, who accepted with an elaborate curtsey she'd learned from Mist.

"Don't say anything on the record," Kelly warned her friend in jest. Then she drifted back a couple of steps to the temporary bar, where Joe was in his usual role operating the tap, and Paul was handling the mixed drinks.

"Party is off to a good start," Joe said. "Is the emperor still busy catching up with his long-lost colonists?"

"He had Libby ping me a few minutes ago to say he'd be back soon and to tell you to save him some beer," Kelly replied. "I haven't seen Beowulf all day either."

"He must be out courting again."

"Is that what you men call it? I just hope that in a couple of months we aren't overwhelmed with legal actions for puppy support."

"Can I get this refilled?" Czeros asked, setting down an empty wine bottle. Paul reached under the table for a new bottle and extracted the cork. "Thank you," the Frunge ambassador enunciated, with the exaggerated care that indicated he'd been drinking for some time.

"Long day, Ambassador?" Joe asked.

"Long night," the Frunge replied, after pausing to take a gulp directly from the bottle. "I've never understood why the Stryx didn't create a standard day and night schedule for the whole station. This business of everybody following their own clocks on their own decks makes it impossible to properly schedule parties."

"But your day is more than twice as long as ours," Kelly pointed out. "Or look at the Verlocks. They intentionally halt the rotation on some of their worlds and just live on the hot side."

Czeros looked at her bleary-eyed. "That's the sort of objection I've grown to expect from a species whose members have more than one name. You like to make things as complicated as possible."

"Good morning," Bork said, winking at Kelly behind the Frunge's back. "I can't really imbibe since I have to go into the office later, but perhaps one Divverflip?"

"Coming up," Paul said, pulling on thick rubber gloves and reaching for the thermos of acid he kept specifically for making Drazen drinks.

"And where is your lovely and talented wife?" Bork asked, while the mixologist donned protective eyewear for in case the reaction was too strong.

"She's recording a special episode at the Empire Convention Center with the children of the open house guests who haven't left yet. None of the local species would agree to have their kids on the same set with those aliens, and the Grenouthians refused to even let them in the studio. But Aisha can be pretty persuasive when she has to be, so the bunnies agreed to try it with a mobile rig."

"Bob Steelforth, Galaxy Free Press. Nobody charged me at the door. Do we pay somewhere for the beer?"

"It's a party, Bob," Kelly replied. "We're sending off the Gem ambassador and her sister, and we're celebrating the end of the open house." The young reporter continued looking at her and nodding, and she realized he was waiting for a definitive answer. "No, you don't pay for the beer."

"Uh oh. Everybody guard your celery," Czeros slurred, and then began laughing at his own joke, which must have been funnier in Frunge.

"Hi, Dring. Have you talked with Gwendolyn and Mist yet?" Kelly asked. The newly arrived Maker eased his way forward between the young reporter and Bork.

"You didn't see me cut in on the dance floor and dip each of them?" the chubby dinosaur replied. He blinked at Kelly's skeptical expression. "Ask Libby for a replay if you don't believe me."

"How come the sentient who lives the closest is always late to the party?" Czeros slurred. He pointed vaguely with his wine bottle in the direction of the Maker's permanent parking space, which was hidden by scrap at the far end of the hold.

"I've just come from the Cayl encampment," Dring said. "Jeeves set them up in Libbyland, on the water treatment deck. It happens that I've visited the home worlds of all five columns at one time or another, but it's the first time in history they're all meeting each other. I don't recall ever hearing of such an event before, where six branches of a species came back together after being out of touch for so long."

"Where's Emperor Brynt?" Kelly asked.

"He was going to stop in at the open house vote on his way back. It's taking place right now in the Thark off-world betting facility."

"And as a historian, you didn't think the vote was worth attending?" Bork asked in surprise.

"I didn't want to miss any more of the party," Dring replied. "Besides, I've attended enough meetings where the representatives of different species were voting on entering or leaving this or that political entity. I could tell you the results without going."

"Do you know something, Dring?" Kelly asked suspiciously.

"I hope I do know something at my age," the Maker replied with dignity.

"You're not going to tell us?"

"It wouldn't be right to scoop Brynt when he took the time to attend the vote," Dring replied.

"Was Jeeves the one who thought of bringing all of those Cayl here?" Bork asked Kelly. "You know we don't usually attempt to pry into Stryx affairs, but this is rather momentous, as Dring pointed out."

"As far as I know, he got the idea after talking with the emperor and Dring at our poker game," Kelly replied. "I have to admit, as much as I like Brynt, the Cayl way of thinking is entirely alien to me."

"Jeeves is a fine young Stryx," Srythlan said ponderously, as he shuffled his way into the conversation. "And I will miss the input of Gwendolyn at our meetings. She is a very sensible sentient."

"For a clone," Czeros added.

"What do you make of the Cayl reunion, my friend?" Dring asked the Verlock ambassador.

"We projected such," Srythlan replied slowly. Dring nodded.

"Did you all see my little girl dance?" Blythe asked proudly. She elbowed through the crowd of ambassadors and passed a couple of Libbyland pilsner glasses to Joe for a refill. "Samuel did great too, but he's not as pretty," she added, for the benefit of the boy's parents.

"If you all crowd around here, nobody else is going to be able to get a drink," Joe remonstrated the growing knot of friends. "We didn't spend half the day putting out tables and chairs just for scenery."

"Clive and the gang grabbed a section near the dance floor," Blythe told them. "Plenty of room for everybody. You guys should have dances more often."

"I remember when this place was a perfectly good junkyard," Joe said to Paul, who nodded in mock seriousness.

"Well, that's where we'll be," Blythe said, accepting the full glasses back from Joe. "Thomas and Chance are in rare form trying to top each other with stories from their early years. They're really a cute couple."

"I'll be right over," Kelly said. "I just want to check with Ian about the catering. I told him to wait a little, in hopes people would dance first."

"Make sure to ask about the celery," Czeros choked out, and this time he began laughing so hysterically that Bork had to grab the Frunge by the elbow to keep him from losing his balance.

Dring shook his head at the inebriated ambassador and led the Verlock off towards the EarthCent Intelligence tables.

A sudden breeze passed over the bar, and movement in her peripheral vision caused the ambassador to look up. Sweeping around for a second pass was the two-man floater manufactured by the humans on Chianga, Jeeves at the controls.

"How did you get it up so high?" Paul called to his Stryx friend. "I thought those floaters had a pretty limited vertical range."

"I improved it," Jeeves said, bringing the craft to a hover beside the bar. "I wanted to license the technology to the Dollnicks, but Gryph squelched the idea. Still, Gwen will have the coolest ride on the Gem home world, and I

226

swapped out the fuel pack with something that will last until well after Mist comes out of stasis."

"You bought the floater for Gwen?" Kelly craned her neck to stare at the Stryx. "I thought you bought it for Libbyland, to make a new ride."

"I bought it because Libby told me you took up a collection to get the Gem ambassador a going-away present but you didn't know what to give her," Jeeves said. "That and the Chiangans gave me a special discount because it had been in a minor accident. Give me the money you collected and you can tell Gwendolyn it's from all of us."

"How much did it cost?"

"Fifteen thousand, plus another two or three for the upgrades. How much did you raise?"

"I'd have to check with Donna," Kelly said evasively.

"Ten thousand?" Jeeves prompted her.

"Maybe not that much," Kelly mumbled.

"Five thousand?"

Kelly grimaced and made the hand movement for "lower" that Joe had taught her to help land small craft flying by visual rules.

"Five hundred?"

"Oh, more than that," Kelly said in relief. "It's just that a lot of the ambassadors still have a thing about clones."

Two huge shapes barreled through the dancers, knocked over some empty chairs, and scrabbled to a halt on either side of the EarthCent ambassador. The latest arrivals were the Cayl emperor and Beowulf, both down on all fours in their "ready" positions. Brynt growled as the dog worked his jaws and swallowed, using Kelly as a shield. Steelforth fumbled with his reporter's tab, trying to capture the action.

"Emperor! What's going on?"

"It was bad enough that he kept sticking his big nose in my snack pouch and stealing biscuits, but this time he's gone too far," Brynt replied. "He bit off half of the ceremonial hardtack baton presented to me by the heads of the five columns."

The Cayl stood up and pulled the remains of a dark brown loaf from his belt. It was long and skinny like a French bread, nicely rounded on one end, and chomped off short on the other.

"The cooks from each column contributed dough made with the sweat from every one of their warriors, and then they baked it with the concentrated light reflected from a hundred shields. It's not intended for eating and I'll be surprised if he doesn't lose a tooth."

Beowulf had thought the strange bread tasted a bit gross, and on hearing why it was so salty, he began to gag and cough.

"Go ahead and give him something to drink," the Cayl told Joe.

The owner of Mac's Bones took the drip pan from under the tap and placed it in front of Beowulf, who lapped up the beer greedily.

"I'm so sorry, Emperor," Kelly said in distress. "He's never stolen food right out of anybody's hands before."

"That's right," Paul added. "He usually relies on bumping into elbows to make the food fall off of people's plates."

Brynt looked down at the remaining half of his hardtack baton and sighed. "I should be apologizing to you. I didn't mean to imply that you did a bad job raising him. My own Gurf once stole the centerpiece from a banquet while we were all looking up to toast the universe. By the time I caught him, he had swallowed half of it down, bones and all."

"Did you punish him?" Joe asked.

"Indigestion punished him. The poor hound was so sick that he wouldn't even eat table scraps for a week."

Beowulf finished lapping up the beer and decided to gamble on coming out from hiding behind Kelly. He put on his most contrite look, kept his head low, and gave his tail an experimental wag. The emperor took Beowulf's massive head in his hands and drew it up near his face. Then he said, "Bad dog," and nipped Beowulf on the muzzle.

The Huravian hound yelped in surprise and sprinted for the ice harvester. He'd never been so embarrassed in his life. The Cayl gave Joe an apologetic shrug.

"He had it coming," Joe agreed.

After she recovered from the unexpected show of imperial dominance, Kelly asked, "What happened at the open house vote?"

"The majority of the emissaries and lesser representatives all voted to join," Brynt replied. "The Lood emissary voted against, and of course, the other species of their faction followed suit. Z'bath made an amusing speech, claiming that his son had been attacked on the station by a Teragram sorceress in human form. Of course nobody took him seriously."

Kelly groaned audibly. "Libby told me that if the vote was in favor, I have to chair a final planning meeting between the emissaries and the local ambassadors who hosted them."

"Most of the open house guests have already departed through the temporary tunnel and the rest will be gone by tomorrow," Jeeves said. Everybody turned to look at the hovering floater. "Before your meeting, we'll deliver a detailed plan for the construction of permanent tunnel connections to the Cayl region of space, a timetable for getting the individual systems hooked up, and a schedule for moving several stations to the region."

"You're going to move whole Stryx stations to Cayl space?" Kelly asked.

"Building a new station takes forever in biological terms, and they're needed to keep the permanent tunnel hubs open," Jeeves explained. "It's all handled by the first-generation Stryx, I'm barely even in the loop, but Gryph asked me to attend your meeting tomorrow in order to manage expectations."

"Tomorrow? I thought you just said something about a detailed plan?"

"Gryph prepared it as soon as the vote was taken," Jeeves replied. "And Stryx Vrine asked me to relay a message from your wife, Emperor. Do you want to hear it now?"

"Does it have to do with the children?" Brynt asked.

"Yes."

"Is somebody hurt, or is she just worried about their futures."

"I would say worried about your oldest son's future."

"Then it can wait until after the party."

"Celery," Czeros declared. He began to laugh hysterically and then passed out in a heap.

Twenty-One

"Thank you all for coming and, um, not spitting." It wasn't how Kelly had intended to open the meeting, but given the way that some of the ambassadors and emissaries were glaring at each other, and the trail of green goo trickling from the mouth opening of the Lood's golden mask, the line just popped into her head. "Stryx Jeeves is here to answer any questions you may have about the proposed infrastructure, and Stryx Gryph will make himself heard if necessary."

"Never mind all of that," Aluria said impatiently, glaring at the emissaries. "Did you believe you could demand a higher price by voting to join?"

"You couldn't pay me to join your tunnel network," the Lood replied haughtily, and then pointed at the Cayl Emperor. "I'm only here because our excursion ships have all departed and he's my ride home."

"How many times have I told you not to point?" Brynt growled at Z'bath.

The Tzvim emissary rose from her seat and went to crouch behind the chairs of the Nangor and the Shuga. The three emissaries put their heads together and held a whispered consultation.

"I don't think we're here for negotiations," Kelly said uncertainly. "My understanding is that the species present will be seeing a lot of each other in the future, and this

231

planning session is to help us coordinate the timetable involved."

"Life is negotiations," the Grenouthian ambassador stated.

"Am I missing something?" Kelly subvoced to Libby. "The vote is over, right? I even made Paul stay up late reading Gryph's infrastructure plan so he could give me an executive summary."

"Some of your colleagues are still hoping to prevent the expansion of the tunnel network for business reasons," Libby replied in Kelly's ear.

"I can see that, but why do they think they can succeed?" Kelly subvoced back. "Will you let them change their votes if they get a big enough bribe?"

"The voting is over, but there are other things they can do."

The three emissaries finally broke their huddle and the Tzvim returned to her seat.

"How much?" Timba asked. He addressed his question to Crute, who happened to be sitting directly across the table from the Nangor. The Dollnick held up two fingers in reply. "And how much from the others?"

"Don't try to be funny," Ortha said. "We've met over this several times and that's our best offer. It's a lot of cash for you in return for not doing anything."

"And what do you offer, Stryx?" Timba inquired, turning towards Jeeves.

"Membership in the tunnel network comes with costs and benefits, as you know," Jeeves replied. "If you'll pull up Exhibit F in the infrastructure plan, I can explain how we plan to position the primary tunnel hubs, given the highly distributed nature of influence in your space."

"I'm not talking about that, Stryx," the Nangor said. "I meant, what will you give us four, well, us three, for going along with your plan?"

"I'm afraid I don't follow you," Jeeves said disingenuously.

"The Dollnicks have come together with the Vergallians, Grenouthians and Hortens to offer us double their GSP to turn down your deal. Clearly that changes our negotiating position."

"What's a GSP?" Kelly subvoced to Libby.

"Gross Species Product," Libby replied. The Grenouthian hopped over to the Dollnick and began whispering urgently, while Aluria leaned in from the other side.

"Nobody offered anybody two times their GSP," Crute said after the brief consultation. "The offer was two billion creds, which I understand will make the four of you some of the richest individuals in the former Cayl Empire."

"That's only because of the fifty-percent tax the Cayl have been assessing on our most successful entrepreneurs each year, a thinly disguised employment program for the poor," Tarngol replied. "Once we're free from the Cayl, those of us with the talent and the work ethic to get ahead will be able to accumulate as much wealth as we desire."

"Putting aside the nonsensical nature of your demands, don't you think you're being extraordinarily greedy?" Aluria inquired in a chilling tone. "After all, we are talking about bribes here. If I choose to have a holo-recording of this meeting sent to your respective governments…"

"All the more reason your offer is insufficient," the Tzvim countered. "If we have to start spreading the money around back home, it's hardly worth the bother."

"Two billion is appreciably more than the Stryx are offering," Ortha pointed out.

All of the diplomats turned again to regard Jeeves, who
floated quietly next to Kelly.

"Is it my turn again already?" the young Stryx asked. "I
bid two yellows."

"Yellow stars?" the Nangor said hopefully. "With habit-
able planets?"

"I think he means poker chips," Kelly said. The Stryx
bobbed in agreement.

"What's a yellow worth?" the Nangor asked.

"Ten millicreds," Kelly replied, bracing herself for the
inevitable explosion.

"So, this whole open house has been a conspiracy to do
us out of our just rewards," Geed declared. "First you
humiliated me by interfering with my private business
transactions, and now you make me an offer that wouldn't
open the pay toilet door on a Wanderer ship. I think I've
seen enough!" The Tzvim rose from the table, turned her
armored back to the gathered diplomats, and began to
stalk away. But she seemed to run out of steam just a few
steps from the table.

"Going somewhere?" the Lood inquired cruelly.

"Looks like somebody just realized she doesn't have a
ride home," the Grenouthian ambassador piled on.

"Alright, we'll take the two billion creds," the Nangor
hissed.

"I'm afraid that offer has sailed," Crute said mildly.
"Allow me to confer with my colleagues."

"Fool!" Tarngol declared, rounding on Timba. "You
should have taken the four-armed freak's offer while it was
good."

"Who are you calling a four-armed freak?" Timba trumpeted, making four fists. The Lood snickered as Brynt pushed between the feuding emissaries, bringing the brawl to a conclusion before it could begin.

"You've embarrassed me in front of Ambassador McAllister and the Stryx for the last time," the Cayl thundered. "The four of you are fired, and you can figure out how to get home by yourselves."

"You can't fire us," Geed retorted. "You're giving up the empire."

"Well, I'm taking it back," Brynt said, and then burst out in hearty laughter. "This whole open house affair was just a ploy to get me to keep the Cayl Empire together, wasn't it, Mr. Jeeves?"

"My elders do seem convinced that your species is the right match for the job," the Stryx replied. "After all, you've been doing it for seven million years, give or take."

"That's it? We don't have to deal with these emissaries again?" Aluria asked.

"They aren't emissaries anymore," Kelly said. "They've been fired."

The four Union Station ambassadors who had hosted the emissaries didn't wait around to hear how things would turn out. The former emissaries slunk out on their heels, leaving Kelly alone with the Cayl emperor and Jeeves.

"I could be angry over your interfering in my plans, Mr. Jeeves," Brynt said. "But my wife has changed her mind about provoking my mother into replacing me, and I owe you for bringing our colonists back into communication. I believe I will contract their services in helping to man our fleet and garrisons. It will give us a reason to reunite, and perhaps it's time we expanded."

"That's the spirit," the young Stryx encouraged the emperor. "Conquer at a loss and make it up in volume."

The EarthCent ambassador's implant pinged with a priority-ten story from the Galactic Free Press, their highest level alert. It was the first time in the three years she had been a subscriber that Kelly had received a top priority notification.

"The Galactic Free Press just released a breaking story that won't push to my heads-up display," Kelly said to Jeeves. Something about the Stryx's lack of surprise made her suspicious. "Are you interfering with my reception?"

"I thought you'd like to see it in high resolution," Jeeves replied, projecting an image of the special edition on the wall.

"Breaking News," Kelly read out loud, "Alien Bites Dog." The accompanying photo showed Brynt holding Beowulf's head and nipping the dog on his muzzle. Below the full color image, credited to Bob Steelforth, the subtitle read, "Cayl Emperor Decides to Keep Empire. Developing Story."

"That's a great picture of me with your dog," Brynt said to the EarthCent ambassador. "Do you think your friend who owns the news business could get me a copy?"

"I'm so sorry," Kelly replied, mistaking the Cayl's response for sarcasm. "There's a human tradition of trying to write shocking headlines from the days when competing newspapers were sold by street-corner hawkers. I don't know how they could have made your decision about preserving the empire a subtitle. I don't even know how they could have found out about it already."

"The Grenouthians began blaring the story a moment after their ambassador left the room," Jeeves said. "Chastity always has somebody monitoring the bunny feed for

236

breaking news, but the Galactic Free Press scooped them with the dog headline. I'm thinking of getting a subscription myself."

"I should go and explain the situation to my Cayl brothers," Brynt said. He came around the table and surprised both Kelly and Jeeves with a hug. "I'm going to miss staying with your family and Beowulf, but it seems that duty requires I prepare for the journey home."

"Are you really going to leave the emissaries behind?" Kelly asked.

"I'd like to, but it wouldn't be fair to the rest of you. Our empire doesn't produce much in the way of diplomats as their services are rarely needed, but I hadn't realized just how bad it's gotten. I should also point out that the citizens who came for the open house were mainly here to dump wealth before the annual tax census. Not exactly the cream of the crop."

"I hope you can stop back home and say goodbye to the children," Kelly said.

"Of course," Brynt reassured her. "I haven't even sent the recall for my shuttle yet. Besides, your husband promised me a lesson on how to brew beer."

......

Back in the ice harvester, Samuel finished filling a large bowl of beer from the current keg on tap. He tiptoed upstairs, checked with Beowulf that the coast was clear, and then headed down the hall to his room.

"Remember, don't let anybody in," the boy instructed the dog as he placed the bowl of beer on the floor. "If Mom comes back and wants to check on me, pretend to have fallen asleep in the doorway."

Beowulf nodded and began lapping up the beer.

Samuel went into his room, rummaged under the bed for the modified suit he'd smuggled home from the Physics Ride, and rapidly put it on over his pajamas. If Jeeves had come through, Ailia was donning a similar suit in the palace on her far-away homeworld. Next, he took his robot souvenir from Libbyland off of the shelf and placed it on the floor facing the largest open area. Finally, he retrieved the control tablet and tapped in the new sequence of symbols Jeeves had shown him. The eyes of the robot glowed green as it established a link with its quantum-coupled mate.

"Samuel? Are you there?" Ailia asked in Vergallian.

"I'm here, but I can't see you," the boy replied in disappointment. "I guess Jeeves couldn't make the suits work."

"I can't put the leggings on over my dress and I didn't want to call my lady-in-waiting to help me take it off, so you'll have to be patient. You wouldn't believe how complicated my clothes are."

"Are you ready yet?" Samuel asked ten seconds later.

"I'll tell you when I am," Ailia replied. "What else is new there?"

"Mist and Gwendolyn are going back to the Gem homeworld so that Mist can sleep until they grow some guy clones for her to date," the boy recounted. "We have the emperor of the Cayl Empire staying with us, and he's really neat, except he makes me eat vegetables. And Dorothy is still dating that boy she found at work."

"Is he nice?" Ailia asked. "Never mind. Of course he's nice or she wouldn't be going out with him."

"He's okay I guess. Are you ready yet? Don't forget the gloves."

"Almost," Ailia replied. There was a pause. "I think I'm ready now. What do I do?"

"Are you holding your control tab?"

"I just picked it up."

"Press the round thing with the weird shape on it, then the thing that looks like a star with planets, then there should be something that looks like me."

"I did," the girl said a few seconds later. "It's asking for a password."

"Jeeves," the boy told her.

"Oh!" Ailia exclaimed, as a full-size hologram of Samuel wearing the Physics Ride suit appeared before her. "Are you seeing me?"

Samuel stepped towards the hologram of Ailia that had appeared in his own room and gave it an experimental poke in the shoulder with his finger.

Ailia gasped, and her head swiveled around as if she expected to see somebody else in the room. "Did you do that?"

"Sure. That's what the suits are for. It wouldn't work otherwise."

Ailia stepped even closer to Samuel's hologram, put her left hand on its right shoulder, and held out her right hand for him to grasp in the classic Vergallian ballroom pose. Samuel carefully put an arm around the waist of the young queen's hologram and took her hand.

"I can feel you," Ailia declared. "Jeeves is a genius."

"He's okay," Samuel allowed grudgingly. "The suits are from Paul's flying ride, but I guess Jeeves did most of the math stuff."

"Crimson Waltz, low volume," Ailia requested, and soft strains of the Vergallian piece began to play in both rooms. Samuel hesitated for a beat, missing the first natural starting point, but then he began to move into the familiar steps that Marcus had taught him to dance with Vivian. The two glided quietly in their own rooms, and since he was leading, it was fortunate that Samuel's room offered less free space than Ailia's or he might have danced her into a wall.

"Your hand should be warm," Ailia said, after the piece reached its end and they stepped apart to bow formally to each other.

"I'll get Banger to ask Jeeves. Do you have time for another dance?"

"Empire of Glory, low volume," Ailia said. Separated by over a thousand light-years, the nine-year-old queen and the ambassador's son matched each other's intricate steps as the music swelled over the little robot's speakers.

Sprawled out in front of the empty bowl and blocking the doorway with his bulk, Beowulf snored and dreamed of chasing pretty Cayl hounds. He caught more than he could count.

EarthCent Ambassador Series:

Date Night on Union Station

Alien Night on Union Station

High Priest on Union Station

Spy Night on Union Station

Carnival on Union Station

Wanderers on Union Station

Vacation on Union Station

Guest Night on Union Station

Word Night on Union Station

Party Night on Union Station

Review Night on Union Station

Family Night on Union Station

Book Night on Union Station

LARP Night on Union Station

About the Author

E. M. Foner lives in Northampton, MA with an imaginary German Shepherd who's been trained to bite bankers. The author welcomes reader comments at e_foner@yahoo.com.

You can sign up for new book announcements on the author's website - IfItBreaks.com

CPSIA information can be obtained
at www.ICGtesting.com
Printed in the USA
BVHW070036200122
626587BV00002B/189